The Three Simple Hard and Fast Rules of The Bachelors' League:

* Never spend the entire night with a woman
* Never share what's on your plate
* Cut her loose after the third date

After eight years of service in the army and one mission gone wrong, the friends of this league are ready to try something new. Termination of their contracts are approved under one condition—each officer owes his commanding officer a favor, and when he calls it in, he expects *complete* <u>unquestioned</u> obedience.

Don't miss:

#255 *The Player*, June 2006
#267 *The Specialist*, September 2006
#283 *The Maverick*, October 2006

"Nelson spins a page-turning delight filled with Southern wit, sizzling sexual tension and a wacky whodunit. The ⬛⬛⬛⬛⬛ peopled wit⬛

—Ro⬛
Th⬛

D0955093

Blaze™

Dear Reader,

Welcome to my MEN OUT OF UNIFORM trilogy! There's something inherently sexy about the cut of Dress Blues, something casually attractive about a set of BDU's. There's honor and courage and the idea of a greater good in every stitch, and those qualities are found in the men who wear them, as well. But if there's anything sexier than a guy *in* uniform, it's a guy *out* of one, and that's what this series is all about.

Jamie Flanagan, Brian Payne and Guy McCann are heroes to die for. They're die-hard bachelors. They're bad boys. They're Southern gentlemen. They're former U.S. Army Rangers. The only way they could be any better would be if they were dipped in chocolate…and since these are Harlequin Blaze stories, that's always a distinct possibility. I hope you enjoy *The Player,* and be sure to check out *The Specialist* coming in September and *The Maverick,* which will be on sale in October. I've paired these guys with heroines who are strong enough to tangle with them, but soft enough to smooth out the rough edges. The result is a series of books that have been fun to write, and rewarding, as well.

I love to hear from my readers, so be sure to pop by my Web site—www.readrhondanelson.com. I blog frequently about the bizarre happenings that make up my everyday life. Sample headings include "The Day My Dog Ate a Glue Stick" and "How I Felled a Possum with a Can of Fruit Cocktail." (See? I told you it was bizarre.)

Happy reading!

Rhonda Nelson

THE PLAYER

Rhonda Nelson

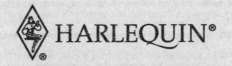

TORONTO • NEW YORK • LONDON
AMSTERDAM • PARIS • SYDNEY • HAMBURG
STOCKHOLM • ATHENS • TOKYO • MILAN • MADRID
PRAGUE • WARSAW • BUDAPEST • AUCKLAND

ISBN 0-373-79259-X

THE PLAYER

Copyright © 2006 by Rhonda Nelson.

All rights reserved. Except for use in any review, the reproduction or utilization of this work in whole or in part in any form by any electronic, mechanical or other means, now known or hereafter invented, including xerography, photocopying and recording, or in any information storage or retrieval system, is forbidden without the written permission of the publisher, Harlequin Enterprises Limited, 225 Duncan Mill Road, Don Mills, Ontario, Canada M3B 3K9.

All characters in this book have no existence outside the imagination of the author and have no relation whatsoever to anyone bearing the same name or names. They are not even distantly inspired by any individual known or unknown to the author, and all incidents are pure invention.

This edition published by arrangement with Harlequin Books S.A.

® and TM are trademarks of the publisher. Trademarks indicated with ® are registered in the United States Patent and Trademark Office, the Canadian Trade Marks Office and in other countries.

www.eHarlequin.com

Printed in U.S.A.

ABOUT THE AUTHOR

A Waldenbooks bestselling author and past RITA® Award nominee, Rhonda Nelson writes hot romantic comedy for the Harlequin Blaze line. In addition to a writing career, she has a husband, two adorable kids, a black Lab and a beautiful bichon frise. She and her family make their chaotic but happy home in a small town in northern Alabama. She's secretly always had a thing for men in uniform and wouldn't object to seeing her husband in a set of BDU's.

Books by Rhonda Nelson

This book is humbly dedicated to all men and women past and present who have served and are currently serving in our armed forces, and to their families who keep the home fires burning.

Prologue

Fort Benning, GA

"WITH ALL DUE RESPECT, sir, that's bullshit."

Colonel Carl Garrett lifted his gaze from the report he'd been pretending to study and determinedly squashed the smile that tried to curl the disapproving line of his lips.

Best not to tip his hand.

Instead, he leveled a cool stare at the three men seated on the wrong side of his desk, most particularly at Guy McCann, who'd issued the comment. The other two, Majors Brian Payne and Jamie Flanagan, sat stony-faced but, predictably, had a better grasp on their tempers.

"Bullshit or not, Lt. Colonel, brawling off-base is an Article 15 and, as I'm sure you're aware, puts a flag on your clearance papers." He paused, purposely injected a little more piss and gravel into his voice. "I'm not sure you're seeing the gravity of the situation."

Not a threat, per se, but a reminder. Hell, he knew perfectly well they understood what was going on. They hadn't been handpicked for Project Chameleon—a special forces unit so secretive that there was absolutely no evidence of its existence in any military file, computer-generated or otherwise—because they were stupid. Garrett suppressed a grimace. In fact, they were too damned smart, which had made trying to get them to rethink leaving the Army with the usual methods—re-upping bonuses, flattery, better posts, etc...—useless.

Unfortunately guilt had a better grasp on them than any form of greed—feeling responsible for the death of a close friend would do that. Through no wrongdoing on their own part, Project Chameleon had lost one of its own during its last mission, and so far, no amount of lecturing and reviewing what had happened could ease their sense of guilt. They'd gone in as four and come out as three.

They'd failed.

Major Payne—a name he'd understandably taken considerable grief for over the years—released a weary breath. "Permission to speak freely, sir?"

"Granted."

"Rutland's an asshole," he said, his voice a barely controlled mixture of irritation and hope. "You know that." He snorted. "Hell, everyone knows that."

"The bastard needed his ass kicked a long time ago," Flanagan chimed in, leaning forward in his seat.

All true, he knew. And he secretly applauded them. Still... "If Rutland needed an attitude adjustment, it was not up to the three of you to give it to him."

"He mouthed off about Danny," Flanagan said, as though that should explain everything.

And it did.

McCann swallowed and the other two grew quiet at the mention of their late friend's name. Silence thick with the weight of grief and regret suddenly expanded in the room, causing a twinge of remorse to prick Garrett's resolve.

Major Daniel Levinson had been a good man, a better soldier, and an original member of this unit's college crew. Each of them had come out of the ROTC program at the University of Alabama. "Roll Tide" was a frequent cheer amid their set and Bear Bryant was revered with the sort of exaggerated regard worthy of a fallen saint. It wasn't merely football—it was a religion.

Though their military careers had taken them on different paths over the years, they'd remained close. Closer than any band or so-called brotherhood of buddies Garrett had ever known. He'd always admired them for that. Truth be told, he'd envied them as well. The military was a boys' club, its very nature a breeding ground for camaraderie and lasting friendships. But these Bama boys were different, had shared a special connection that made them more like family than friends.

When Project Chameleon had come along, it had been a no-brainer to reunite the four. They'd all been at the top of their field, each one of them successful in their own right. Each one of them different enough to offer unique qualities to the unit, making it one of the most balanced and effective special forces teams the Army had ever known.

Though he had a reputation for being a bit of a ladies' man—a *player* in today's slang, if Garrett remembered correctly—at a little over six and half feet, Flanagan not only had the brawn but also sported a genius-level IQ which made him the brain of the unit. Honestly, it had surprised him to learn that Flanagan had thrown the first punch in this recent scuffle. Ordinarily he wasn't quite so rash. Though they'd all taken Levinson's death hard, Garrett suspected that Flanagan was having a harder time dealing with the loss than the other two at the moment.

Understandable, of course, given how Danny had died. Still...

With nerves of steel and an attention-to-detail which had landed him the nickname "The Specialist," Major Brian Payne—who only went by his last name—didn't do anything in half-baked, half-assed measures. He was a man you could count on to not only get the job done, but get it done *right.*

Guy McCann was a bit of a smart-ass with an endearing penchant for being able to bend a rule just shy of the breaking point, but with good enough instincts that he always landed on his feet. And Levinson... Well, Levinson had been the best of all three, and what he'd lacked he'd made up for in heart.

On their own they'd been formidable defenders of Uncle Sam—together they'd been lethal.

Naturally when the powers-that-be had heard rumors of their intent to leave, he'd been given strict instruction to prevent it. Garrett ran a finger over the flag attached to the topmost file. They'd inadvertently given him the power to do it, and yet, when it had come down to the nut-cutting, he'd been unable to follow through. Better to have them in his debt than have an unwilling unit too bent on leaving to be effective. Better a grateful man than a bitter soldier. If they were bound and determined to leave—and they were—then if he could wring one more mission, be it personal or professional, out of them, then he'd still be better off. Fortunately the brass above him had thought so as well.

"So what's going to happen?" Guy asked. "How long is this going to hold us up?"

"That depends," Garrett told them, leaning back in his chair.

Guy's green gaze sharpened. "On what?"

"On whether or not you agree to my terms."

The three of them stiffened and shared a guarded look. "*Your* terms?" Guy asked warily. A muscle ticked in his tense jaw.

At last…the heart of the matter, Garrett thought. "That's right. You want out. We can do this one of two ways. The hard way… Or my way."

Flanagan muttered a hot oath, leaned back and

shoved a hand through his dark brown hair. "I knew this was going to happen," he said, shooting Guy a dark look. "We're *so* screwed."

"Sonofabitch," Guy muttered angrily.

Payne swallowed what was most likely a similar statement, but managed to hold his temper. Just barely, judging by the vein throbbing in his forehead. "And what, exactly, would *your* way entail?" he asked.

"Nothing complicated," Garrett told them smoothly. "You'll just owe me."

"Owe you?" Guy repeated, with equal amounts of surprise and trepidation.

Jamie frowned, his hazel eyes wary. "Owe you what?"

Garrett shrugged, but his tone belied the casual gesture. "A favor." He cast them all a steely look in turn. "From each of you. When I call it in, I want no questions asked, no excuses. Just do it."

Guy considered him with a measuring, probing look. "That calls for a lot of trust."

"I've worked with you for the past four years, McCann. It's either there or it isn't. The choice is yours."

A beat slid into five while the three of them shared another one of those unspoken looks of communication. Garrett watched closely, but didn't detect a single indication of yea or nay from any one of them. Yet Payne evidently got the message because it was he who ultimately spoke for the group. "One favor from each of us? That's it?"

Garrett nodded, anticipation spiking.

Payne released an even breath. "Then we accept your terms, sir. We want out. If you can make that happen quickly, then a favor won't be a problem."

"Excellent," Garrett told them, his lips curling into a belated smile. "Consider it done."

The three stood, preparing to leave. Garrett found his feet as well and extended his hand to each of them, sealing their bargain with a handshake. An old-fashioned gesture, but one that was better than a contract with men like these. They were men of courage, dignity and honor. A rare breed in this day and age.

He let go a sigh, fully absorbing the fact that they would no longer be under his command and found himself quite startled to realize that he'd…miss them. He cleared his throat. "Gentlemen, it's been a pleasure."

"Likewise, sir," Flanagan told him.

"An honor," McCann added.

A man of few words, Payne merely shot him a look which aptly conveyed the same sentiment, then added, "Until later, sir."

Garrett felt a grin tug at his lips. "Oh, don't worry," he told them. "I'll be in touch."

"WHAT THE HELL WAS THAT all about?" Guy asked as they made their way down the hall away from Garrett's office.

"Leverage," Jamie said grimly, feeling an immeasurable amount of relief regardless of the bargain he'd just made. It was over. Finished. Ranger Security—their postmilitary plan—was, at most, a mere month away, and it couldn't come a day sooner. In fact, he would have just about promised Garrett anything—a firstborn, his left nut, hell *anything*—to have pushed those clearance papers through.

He wanted out. End of story.

Jamie shot Payne a look. "What's your take on this favor bargain?"

Payne cocked a brow and shoved open the front doors, revealing the beautiful natural landscape of Fort Benning proper. Georgia, he thought. God's country. "I think Garrett's a crafty bastard who just secured three freebies for Uncle Sam."

"Or for himself," Guy drawled. "He wasn't very specific. Hell, for all we know we could end up being his personal errand boys."

"What? And waste all our special training?" Jamie chewed the inside of his cheek and shook his head. "He might have something personal in mind, but you can bet your sweet ass it's going to be something which requires our particular set of skills."

Guy inclined his head at the point, then blew out a breath. "Well, frankly I don't give a damn what he wants—I'm just glad it's over."

Now that was a sentiment they all shared. Jamie felt a crooked smile slide across his lips, looked over and caught the vaguest hint of a grin transform Payne's usually impassive countenance.

"Boys," Guy said meaningfully, "I say it's time to celebrate."

Payne nodded once in agreement. "I wouldn't say no to a cold one."

Jamie hesitated, wincing. He was about to severely tick off his friends and he knew it.

Guy glanced at him and frowned. "Let me guess," he said, his lips twisted with sarcastic humor. "I'm going to take a shot in the dark here and say that you've got a date."

"With Michelle," Jamie admitted.

"Date three, right?" Payne asked.

Jamie chewed the corner of his lip and nodded.

"Ah," Guy sighed knowingly. "Then she'll be getting the Sayonara Serenade?"

"Of course." Rather than linger and feel their censure—Payne, in particular had become annoyingly vocal on the amount of time he chose to spend with the opposite sex of late—Jamie turned and started walking backward toward his jeep. "Cold beer or a warm woman?" He chuckled, lightening the moment. "It's an easy choice, guys."

Or at least it was for him.

GUY MCCANN WATCHED AS Jamie cranked his jeep and, wearing a cocky I'm-getting-laid grin, drove off.

How Jamie got a woman to sleep with him *after* he'd officially cut her loose was a phenomenon that both Guy and Payne had marveled over for years. Especially since it had been Jamie's love life that had necessitated setting up some rules. After a particularly bad breakup, Guy, Payne and Jamie had sat down over beers and decided on three hard and fast mandates for preserving their bachelor status.

Frankly, he and Payne had personal reasons for wanting to remain single, but Jamie had always been the romantic of the three. At least until he'd caught Shelly Edwards, the so-called love of his life, balling their landlord in lieu of rent.

In their bed, no less.

At any rate, after that particularly humiliating episode Jamie had changed. Instead of looking for the love of his life, he'd merely started looking for the love of his *night*. Following their rules—never spend the entire night with a woman, never let her eat off your plate, and after the third date, cut her loose—he'd pretty much perfected what they'd dubbed "kamikaze romance." After all, every relationship was destined to crash and burn.

Payne watched him drive away as well, then glanced at Guy. "Is it just me, or is he getting worse?"

"Getting worse?"

"More women, more often."

Guy mulled it over, rubbed the back of his neck. Actually, he hadn't noticed, but now that Payne had pointed it out, it did seem like Jamie hadn't been around as much lately. Aside from making plans for Ranger Security, Jamie hadn't had much time for their usual pursuits—beer, poker, target practice, etc… In fact, now that he really thought about it, Jamie's dating schedule had taken a dramatic upswing in the months since Danny's death.

He looked up and caught Payne's knowing gaze. "I see you've come to the same conclusion that I did," Payne told him.

Guy nodded, his mood suddenly somber. "Getting out will help," he said. It had to. And God knows that was the truth for him. There wasn't a day that went by that he didn't think about Danny, about the part he played in his friend's death. If he'd only… Aw, hell, Guy thought, abruptly shutting down that line of thinking.

He could "if-only" until hell froze over and the outcome would still be the same—Danny Levinson, best friend, beloved son, brother, uncle and cousin to a family which still grieved his loss, would still be six feet under in Arlington National Cemetery.

He'd still be gone.

And no matter what Garrett, Payne or Jamie ever said, Guy knew he'd never stop believing that it was his fault. As the senior officer, he'd been in charge. He couldn't take credit for the success of the mission without also taking blame for the loss. And no one would ever convince him otherwise.

It was that simple…and that complicated.

For the time being, they were each three days and three favors away from freedom—a brand-new life devoid of mistakes and if-onlys—and God knows they all needed it. Especially Jamie, who seemed to be taking it the hardest. An image of Danny's crooked grin suddenly rose in his mind, causing a barbed-wire of tension to tighten around his chest.

They all needed it, all right. They needed it badly.

1

"IT'S HAPPENED," Jamie Flanagan announced grimly. He snagged a chair from a nearby table, whirled it around and straddled it with a dejected whoosh of air that effectively caught his best friends' combined attention.

In the process of licking the hot wing sauce from his fingertips, Guy looked up. "Dammit, we both warned you about this. Which one is pregnant? Christy? Liz? Monica?"

"My money's on Monica," Payne said easily. "She was clingy."

"Had to change the security code to the building because of her, remember?"

Payne nodded, absently taking a pull from his beer. "She was a pain in the ass, I remember that."

Guy shot Jamie a pleading look. "It isn't her, is it, Flanagan? Say it isn't her. She's, er… She's not mother material."

Equally annoyed and horrified, Jamie swore hotly. He should have known they'd leap to the wrong damned conclusion. Considering they'd both been riding his ass about his "serial" dating, it only stood to reason that they'd immediately suspect a woman problem.

"Nobody's pregnant, dammit," he snapped. "How many times do I have to tell you bastards that I'm careful?" He exhaled loudly. "I know how to apply a friggin' rubber, for chrissakes. It's Garrett. He's calling in my *favor.*"

Guy blinked. "Oh."

Payne stilled and his ice-blue gaze sharpened. "What does he want?"

Jamie let out another long breath, uttered a short disbelieving laugh and shook his head. "He wants me to go to Maine for a week to guard his granddaughter."

"Guard his granddaughter?" Payne repeated. "Guard her from what?"

That had been the first question he'd asked as well, and the answer he'd gotten had been irritatingly ambiguous. Not that he hadn't taken and followed orders on less information. He'd been trained to obey, to trust in the authority of his superiors, and yet something about this felt...*off*. He'd tried to chalk it up to his new civilian mentality, but he suspected that this gut hunch had more to do with intuition than new programming.

"Garrett says there's evidence that a personal enemy of his might be targeting her."

Guy frowned. "Personal enemy?"

"What sort of personal enemy?" Payne asked. "I mean, I don't doubt that he's got one—a man doesn't get to his level without pissing people off. Still..." he added skeptically.

Jamie couldn't help scowling. "That's just it. He wouldn't say. Evidently he's got someone in place through the weekend, but needs me to step in on Monday."

"We'll have to rearrange some things," Payne said, predictably jumping into logistics mode. "Guy and I will have to split your cases."

"It's piss-poor timing, that's for sure," Jamie said, signaling the waitress for a beer. A midtown staple, Samuel's Pub had quickly become their traditional beer and sandwich haunt. Good Irish whiskey, good prices, Braves decor. What more could a guy want? Jamie muttered a hot oath. "Hell, some notice would have been nice."

Guy rocked back in his chair and grinned. "But that would be completely out of character for Garrett."

Too true, Jamie knew, but it didn't change the fact that he'd be leaving his friends and partners in the lurch three months out of the gate in their new business venture. Thanks in part to all three of them, Ranger Security had taken off better than any one of them could have expected. Jamie inwardly grinned. Turns out hi-tech personal and professional security was in high demand—and quite lucrative.

Thanks to Payne's investment capital—though he seemed to resent his impressive portfolio at times, Payne had "come from money" as Jamie's grandmother used to say—they'd secured top-of-the-line equipment and a prized office building in downtown Atlanta. The lower level housed the offices and the other two floors had been converted into apartments. Since he and Guy had no aversion to sharing space, they'd taken the second floor and Payne had moved into the loft, or the Tower, as they'd come to call it.

Since Payne had taken on so much of the financial burden, it only seemed fair that he have a place to himself. Not that Jamie and Guy weren't paying their way, but their money had come from a sizable mortgage whereas Payne had merely "transferred funds." Regardless, provided business continued to grow, he and Guy should be operating in the black within a few years, and in his opinion, that was pretty damned good.

"So the granddaughter is in Maine," Guy remarked. "What does she do?"

Ah, Jamie thought, inwardly wincing. Here came the fun part. He passed a hand over his face and braced himself for sarcasm. "She, er… She runs a de-stressing camp for burned out execs— Unwind, it's called—and well, Garrett's, uh…" He conjured a pained smile. "He's already arranged for my 'stay.'"

A disbelieving chuckle erupted from Guy's throat. "A de-stressing camp? He's sending *you*— Captain Orgasm—to a de-stressing camp?"

Payne coughed to hide his own smile. "To guard his granddaughter, no less. Talk about sending the fox in to guard the henhouse." He snorted. "Garrett must have lost his mind."

"Oh, no," Jamie corrected. "He's as crafty as ever. He issued a curt guard-her-but-no-funny-business order and promised to—" Jamie pretended to search for the exact phrase, though he remembered the ghastly threat verbatim. "Ah, yes. 'Cut my dick off with a dull axe and force-feed it to me' if I so much as looked at her with anything more than friendly interest."

Payne grinned. "So your reputation precedes you, then."

Jamie winced. "He might have mentioned Colonel Jessup's daughter."

And honestly, there had been no need. After that horrid debacle, Jamie hadn't needed any additional threats to stay away from daughters—or any relative, for that matter—belonging to superior officers. And it really wouldn't be hard. There were plenty of other available women around.

Neesa Jessup had seduced *him*, not the other way around, and yet when Date Three had rolled around and he'd attempted to break things off, she'd gone to her father and cried foul. It had been a huge ugly mess and, given his particular reputation, no one was readily inclined to believe him. Guy, Payne and Danny had, of course, but they'd been on a short list. Needless to say, since then he'd been a lot more…selective.

Payne took another mouthful of beer and swallowed. "So I take it you're going in undercover?"

Jamie nodded. "That's the plan."

"I still don't get it," Guy said, his shrewd gaze speculative. "How are you supposed to guard her if you don't know where the threat is coming from?"

Precisely, Jamie thought, still smelling a rat. "He told me he'd give me an update once I'm in place, but the gist of the order was to stick to her like glue."

Guy scowled. "And that's not going to look suspicious?"

Jamie shrugged. Just thinking about it made his head hurt. "Hell if I know," he muttered tiredly. It sounded odd, but not altogether difficult, so that was a plus, right? In all honesty, it would be a relief to simply be done with it. This favor was his last niggling tie to a life he'd left behind. Had to leave behind to preserve his own sanity.

Even as early as last year, if anyone had told him that he'd wanted to be anything other than a United States Army Ranger, he would never have believed it. The military had given him purpose, manned him up and given him an outlet for what he now recognized as disappointment toward an absentee father.

Thanks to a hardworking mother and a hot-headed Irish grandmother who weren't averse to boxing his ears when the need arose—an unexpected smile curled his lips, remembering—Jamie had been a lot better off than a lot of the boys he knew whose fathers *had* been around.

Like Guy, Jamie thought, covertly shooting a look at his friend. Guy's old man had been a royal bastard, a hard-assed proponent of the "spare the rod, spoil the child" mentality. Unfortunately that had been the extent of his religious tendencies. He'd been a mean-spirited drunk who, on more than one occasion, had sent his son to the Emergency Room. Guy hadn't heard from the man since he was in his late teens. Frankly, Jamie had toyed with the idea of looking the old man up and thrashing the shit out of him. Someone needed to, at any rate.

Jamie's gaze slid to Payne. Payne's father had been at home while Payne was growing up, but from the little things that his friend had shared over the years, he might as well have not been. Payne's father had always had one eye on the door and the other on another woman. His parents had apparently stayed married for Payne's benefit, but Jamie suspected Payne would have had a lot more respect for both of them if they'd merely divorced and done away with the infidelities.

They finally ended the marriage when Payne graduated from high school and since then, Payne's father had systematically married and divorced women who were craftily garnering another portion of his inheritance. He needed to be thrashed as well, Jamie decided, but for different reasons.

Quite frankly, all three of them had been raised in unconventional households and the older Jamie got, the more he suspected that no one's family was normal. Normal was as real as Santa Claus and the Tooth Fairy.

Normal didn't exist.

And after Danny's death, he wasn't so sure that the ideas of *right* and *just* weren't myths also. If they existed, if they were true, then why hadn't Danny walked away from that ill-fated mission with the rest of them?

Being in the military, death was a distinct possibility. One didn't enlist without knowing—without *believing*—in the greater good and being willing to die for that cause. Jamie, Guy, Payne, Danny—they'd all felt the same way.

Being a Ranger was more than a career. It had

been a labor of love. Brave men had essentially committed treason when they'd formed this country. Thomas Jefferson had been in his early thirties when he'd penned the Declaration of Independence. That still amazed him, Jamie thought. So young and yet so wise. A vastly different world and set of values from where they were today. But that was a whole other issue.

At any rate, their very freedom was based on bravery, on loyalty and on a belief in a cause that so many, quite frankly, didn't appreciate and took for granted. There were thousands of men in marked and unmarked graves all over the globe who'd boldly gone to war and sacrificed their lives for this country. Jamie would gladly give his own…and yet living with the grief of a fallen friend somehow seemed more difficult than dying himself.

Something had changed that night. Not just for him, but for Guy and Payne as well. Rationally they'd all known the risks. But knowing it and dealing with it had turned out to be two completely different things. Did Jamie still believe in his country? In his service? In the merit of even that particular mission?

Yes, to all of the above.

He just didn't believe he could watch another friend die.

Danny, a brother to him in every way that counted, had taken his last breath in Jamie's arms. He'd watched the spark fade from Dan's eyes, felt his life slip away like a shadow…and Jamie had felt a part of himself die on that sandy, blood-soaked hill as well.

The familiar weight of grief filled his chest, forcing him to release a small breath. Whatever Garrett wanted him to do had to be easier than that, by God. It had to be.

"Look at it this way," Guy finally said in a blatant attempt to lighten the moment when the silence had stretched beyond the comfortable, a still too often occurrence. He shrugged. "She could be ugly."

Payne nodded, smiling encouragingly. "It'd definitely be easier for you to guard an ugly woman, Flanagan. Less temptation." He selected a celery stick. "What's her name?"

Smiling in spite of himself, Jamie rubbed the bridge of his nose. "Audrey Kincaid."

"Pretty name," Guy remarked thoughtfully. "But that doesn't mean anything," he added magnanimously, the smart-ass.

"Right," Payne said. "She could still be ugly."

Not even with the luck of the Irish, Jamie thought, but it didn't matter. She could look like a friggin' supermodel and he wasn't going to touch her with a ten-foot pole.

Actually, he had a grim suspicion who the granddaughter might be and he knew for a fact that not only wasn't she ugly, but in fact, she was drop-dead instant-hard-on gorgeous. The Colonel only had two pictures of family in his office—one Jamie knew for a fact was Garrett's wife because he'd met her several times.

The other was of a young blue-eyed beauty about the right age with long curly black hair. It was a candid shot of her and an enormous brindled English Mastiff. Considering the dog wasn't lunging for her throat, but sitting docilely by her side, Jamie could only assume the animal was hers.

His lips quirked. Quite frankly, if that was who he was being sent to protect, he imagined the dog could do a better job of it than he could. Furthermore, he hoped like hell it wasn't her, because for reasons he'd never really understood, he'd always been drawn to that picture, of the woman in it specifically. Every time he'd visited Garrett's office he found himself staring at it—at *her*. There was an inherent kindness in her eyes, a softness about her that he found particularly compelling. That trait combined with the obvious intelligence and just a hint of mischief made her face the most interestingly beautiful one he'd ever seen.

No doubt guarding her would be absolute torture, particularly given Garrett's orders. Jamie felt a grin tease his lips. He was pretty attached to his penis, thank you very much, and there wasn't a doubt in his mind that Garrett wouldn't make good on his threat if Jamie put so much as a toe out of line.

Furthermore, if he botched this favor, he'd just end up owing Garrett another one and moving on would be that much further away. Jamie tipped his tumbler back, felt the smooth amber taste slide down his throat.

And there wasn't a woman alive who could make him risk that.

2

CELL PHONE SHOULDERED to her ear, Audrey Kincaid stood at the cashier's stand of her local grocery store, absently pulled a tampon out of her purse and tried to write a check with it.

The thin, pimply-faced teenager behind the register sniggered. "Er... That's not going to work, ma'am."

Mortified, Audrey closed her eyes and, blushing furiously, awkwardly shoved her hand back into her bag in search of a pen. Ordinarily she thought it was incredibly rude of people to use their cell phones while in the checkout and, had she been talking to anyone but her grandfather, she would have cut the call short, or merely asked the person to call back.

But one didn't do that with her grandfather.

The Colonel didn't abide interruptions.

He was accustomed to being listened to and the

idea that she—or any one else for that matter—
might not be interested in what he had to say was
unthinkable. A military man through and through,
he was a surly, autocratic, occasionally ill-tem-
pered pain in the ass who thought that an untucked
shirttail was an abomination and rap music a crime
against nature. His vehicles were American made,
his lawn an immaculate work of art where the grass
didn't dare offend him by growing out of sync, and
his home office an inner sanctum of dark wood,
Old Spice and the scent of cherry cigar smoke.

Though he was the unquestioned leader of their
family, most of the members of their clan could
only tolerate him in small doses, her mother
included. But for whatever reason, he and Audrey
had always shared a special bond. For all of his
grit and grump, from the time she'd been just a
little girl she'd loved listening to his stories. While
the other grandchildren had gravitated to their
grandmother's sewing room and kitchen, Audrey
had preferred playing chess in the Colonel's office
and coaxing orchids and other finicky flowers in
his greenhouse.

Was now a bad time to talk? Definitely. She was
standing in the checkout, feeling the murderous
eye of a harried mother behind her, trying to write

a damned check with a tampon, for pity's sake…
but she had no intention of letting him know that.
She had neither the nerve nor the disrespect to pull
it off.

"I need a favor, Audie," her grandfather said,
using the nickname he'd given her shortly after she
was born.

Audrey handed the cashier a check, accepted
her receipt and one-handedly wheeled her cart-
with-the-cockeyed-wheel toward the door. No
small feat, she thought, suppressing an irritated
grunt. Trying to sound as though she wasn't the
least bit inconvenienced, she said, "Sure, Gramps.
What can I do for you?"

"I'm sending a guy to you who's in need of
special attention."

Her grandfather referring someone to Unwind—
her camp for the stressed-out from all walks of life,
whether it was high-powered executives who'd
logged in too many hours and consumed too many
antidepressants, or strung-out mothers who'd doled
out too many juice boxes and covered car-pool one
time too many—wasn't the least bit unusual. She'd
had many a weary soldier through her camp, many
an overwhelmed officer's wife ensconced in one of
her little lakeside cottages.

But this was the first time he'd ever asked her to give anyone *special* attention. Clearly, this was no ordinary person. Whoever this guy was, given her grandfather's line of work, he'd most likely been through hell. Her heart inexplicably squeezed for both the unknown man and his unknown pain.

Empathy, dammit. Her biggest weakness.

Four years into a high-powered job on Wall Street as a commodities broker, Audrey had had the ultimate wake-up call—at the ripe old age of twenty-six, she'd had a heart attack. A small one, but still a heart attack nonetheless. She'd been healthy—a regular at the gym—with no prior history of any cardiovascular problems.

In the weeks preceeding it, however, she'd had multiple stress-related panic attacks, had started filling her regular thirty-two-ounce java cup with straight-up espresso and her snack of choice had been chocolate-covered coffee beans. Hell, she'd been wound so tight it had been a miracle that she hadn't snapped completely.

To make matters worse, she'd been in a bad relationship which had ended with a restraining order. Unfortunately, Audrey had a knack for attracting damaged men who needed a lot of attention—emotional vampires, she'd come to call them, because they tended to suck the life right out of her.

But no more.

She'd promised herself after Jerry that she'd never get involved with another damaged, life-sucker again. A wry smile curled her lips.

And her present boyfriend was anything but that.

At any rate, she'd had to seriously rethink her life path and the first thing that her family—and her grandfather, in particular—had insisted she do was give up the job. Initially Audrey had protested. What the *hell* was she supposed to do? But one teary-eyed look from the Colonel, when she would have sworn the man had had his tear ducts surgically removed, had been all it took to make her seek an alternate, less stressful career.

After her own heart attack, Audrey had learned that there were many more like her—young Type-A professionals who were burning the candle at both ends and essentially stressing their healthy bodies beyond their limits. When a well-meaning friend suggested that she make a list of things that relaxed her, then take it with her to a soothing vacation spot, a lightbulb went off for Audrey and Unwind was born.

She took a risk, cashed in her 401-K, and bought a somewhat run-down thirty-two-acre summer sleep-away camp up on Lake Bliss in Winnisauga, Maine. A year later Unwind was a fully renovated quaint, but comfortable getaway with custom luxuries for each of its visitors.

Two years after that, it was operating fully in the black.

In order to personalize each experience, campers were required to fill out a lengthy questionnaire which detailed the reason for their visit as well as personal preferences for their ultimate relaxing stay. She had a fabulous kitchen crew on staff as well as a fully-equipped spa. The library sported hundreds of books and movies for campers who craved brain candy and mindless entertainment.

For those who liked to work out their frustrations in a more physical manner, there were the stables, a state-of-the-art gym, various hiking trails and a multitude of water sports compliments of the lake. Between the amenities which were automatically provided and the accommodations she made as a result of the campers' requests, Unwind provided a calm, soothing atmosphere of escape and relaxation. In short, it was the baby of her own rebirth and she loved it.

Audrey opened the back gate of her SUV and began loading her grocery bags into the cargo area.

"I've already spoken to Tewanda," her grandfather said, "and took the liberty of filling out all the necessary paperwork."

In the process of awkwardly moving a twenty-pound bag of dog food—which would last all of one week the way that Moses, her English Mastiff, ate—Audrey frowned. "*You* filled out the paperwork?"

He hesitated. "Flanagan will be there on my orders and I'm not altogether sure he would have been completely truthful regarding the nature of his visit."

That made sense, she supposed. Despite her best efforts to draw people out, they were often purposely vague about the reason for their visit. Still, part of the Unwind experience was customization. How was she supposed to customize this visit if the participant hadn't filled out the form? Tewanda knew this, Audrey thought. Surely her crackerjack assistant hadn't simply let that slide. Even for her grandfather. Oh, hell. Who was she kidding? *She* wouldn't have called him on it. How could she expect Tewanda to?

Thoroughly intrigued now, Audrey closed the back gate and climbed into the driver's seat. "And what exactly is the reason for his visit?"

"He lost a good friend eight months ago," the Colonel said somberly. "Let's just say that he's having a hard time getting through it."

Audrey's heart squeezed. "That's certainly understandable."

Her grandfather cleared his throat. "Right. Well, it would probably be better if you didn't mention it to him. He just needs some TLC and no one can give him that quite the way that you can, Audie. You have a rare gift for making people feel better."

Gift or curse? Audrey wondered, more often feeling like it was the latter. She'd always been a very empathetic person, to the point that she often absorbed so much of another person's pain that she made herself physically ill. Even as a little girl she'd managed to attract the downtrodden, the kids everyone picked on. In her teens, things had pretty much stayed the same—the rebels, the outcasts, the shy and withdrawn. Basically anyone with a problem.

But with maturity came a different set of issues, bigger obstacles, and she found herself staying emotionally wrung out. She'd given so much to other people—usually, and to her detriment, to a significant other—that she hadn't had anything left for herself. Unwind had been the perfect solution because it had afforded her the opportunity to capitalize on her strengths, but enabled her to share the load, so to speak.

"What was his name again?" she asked. She wanted to make sure to look for the paperwork when she got back to camp.

"Major Jamie Flanagan. He was a Ranger in a special forces unit of mine. A damn fine one," her grandfather added with obvious pride.

"*Was* a Ranger?"

"Er… He and a couple of other friends left the military a few months ago."

Audrey paused. She didn't understand. If he'd left the military, then how could her grandfather *order* him into Unwind? "But—"

Accurately following her line of thinking, the Colonel chuckled. "What?" he joked. "You think a soldier who leaves the military automatically leaves my command, Audie?" She could almost see him shaking his head. "Surely you know me better than that?"

One would think so, Audrey thought. Her grandfather…you had to love him.

"Anyway, enough about Flanagan. He'll be arriving Monday and I've made sure that I've listed activities which should—" he cleared his throat of a distinctly wicked chuckle "—*appeal* to him. All I ask is that you keep a close eye on him. Spend as much time with him as possible. I'll call for regular updates on his progress."

This conversation was getting weirder and weirder by the second. One minute her grandfather sounded genuinely concerned, the next he sounded downright…gleeful. She'd better take a look at that questionnaire, Audrey thought with a curious sense of foreboding. Something definitely wasn't right.

"So tell me what's happening with you?" he asked briskly, effectively ending that line of conversation. "Still seeing David?"

"It's Derrick," Audrey replied, repressing a smile. Her grandfather knew this perfectly well. He just couldn't stand the guy. "And yes, I am."

"More's the pity," her grandfather said glibly, never one to mince words. And unfortunately he had many where Derrick was concerned.

Audrey exhaled a long-suffering sigh. *"Gramps,"* she chided.

"You could do so much better, you know. You're a smart, pretty girl. Why you'd want to shackle yourself to that self-absorbed blowhard for the rest of your life is a mystery to me."

A frown wrinkled her brow. She hadn't told her family that Derrick had proposed. "Who said I was getting married?"

"No one," he said. Almost too easily, Audrey thought, wondering if she was being a tad paranoid. "I just assumed that since you're still together, marriage has to be on the horizon. What's the point of a prolonged relationship if you aren't moving toward a more permanent arrangement? If there's no goal, there's no point, right?"

For someone who didn't like Derrick, her grandfather had an alarmingly similar thought process. Derrick had used the same argument just last week when he'd issued his ultimatum—marry him or break up.

Quite frankly, she didn't want to do either.

For reasons she knew better than to explore, marrying him right now was out of the question… But she didn't want to break up either. Sure Derrick had his faults. He spent too much time on his hair, he laughed too hard at his own jokes and, the biggest turnoff of all, he screamed like a girl when he came. This high-pitched, rupture-your-eardrums screech would be right at home in a bad B-movie. Honestly, it was awful.

In addition, he was *a bit* self-absorbed, but that only meant that he wasn't dependent upon her to fill him up, right? After a succession of life-suckers, that had certainly been a welcome change, one that she'd desperately needed.

While she could admit that his confidence might get on other people's nerves, most of the time it didn't bother her at all. Really. She told herself that it was refreshing, that confidence was an admirable trait and Derrick... She grinned in spite of herself. Well, Derrick had that particular characteristic in spades.

Which is why her grandfather hated him.

Her lips curled with wry humor. Evidently her grandfather didn't think Derrick had the necessary qualities to back up the confidence. But it didn't matter what her grandfather thought. It only mattered what Audrey thought, and most of the time Derrick's somewhat exaggerated ego didn't bother her at all. There was something to be said for a guy who wasn't dependent on her opinion. Compared to her other relationships, Derrick was a walk in the park. He was easy.

Was she in love with him? Probably not. Her

heart didn't skip a beat when he touched her hand—
or any other part of her, for that matter—and,
though he traveled frequently with his job, she
couldn't exactly say that she'd ever truly missed
him.

But there was a consistency and predictability
to their relationship which she found quite comfortable, for lack of a better explanation. And she
had no desire to change the status quo. Hopefully
by the end of next week she'd be able to come up
with a convincing argument for her cause. That
was the plan, at any rate, as far as she had one.

"Well, you know what I think of him," her
grandfather said. "He's a—"

Audrey chuckled softly. "Yes, Gramps, I certainly don't have to wonder about that." Ever. In
fact, she could confidently say that not many
people *ever* had to wonder what the Colonel
thought. It was part of his charm.

"Don't be fresh, young lady," he scolded. "I
only have your best interests at heart. And he's not
one deserving of yours," he added gruffly.

Affection swelled, making Audrey smile. Now
how could she stay mad at him when he said
things like that? "I know you do."

"Yeah, well, always be sure and keep that in

mind," he muttered darkly, causing a momentary premonition of dread.

Audrey scowled. "Why would I need to keep that—"

"Gotta go, sweetheart," he said briskly. "Your grandmother's got dinner on the table and you know how she gets if the roast gets cold. I'll talk to you next week. Take good care of my boy." A resounding click echoed into her ear, signaling the end of their bizarre conversation.

Baffled, Audrey stared at her cell before closing it, then gave her head a little shake. Men, she thought. Even the older, so-called wiser ones were incomprehensible.

In future, keep that in mind, he'd said. Clearly he intended to give her a reason to do just that.

The question was…*what?*

3

"LET ME GET THIS STRAIGHT," the young Halle Berry look-alike on the other side of the reception desk said. "*You're* the Colonel's friend?" She had an "oh-hell-no" look on her face, as if she couldn't quite believe him.

Jamie smiled awkwardly. "I am," he repeated, verifying the fact.

Her dark brown eyes widened in what could only be described as shocked disbelief, then her gaze turned consideringly crafty and a secret smile curled her lips. "That sly old dog," she muttered under her breath, flipping through a stack of large white envelopes. "He said he had an ace up his sleeve, but I never dreamed…" She trailed off.

"I'm sorry?"

She looked up and handed him a packet. "Oh, nothing." She smiled warmly. "Welcome to Unwind. I'm Tewanda. If you have any questions, you can reach me by dialing zero from the phone in your cottage. Here's your welcome information as well as your itinerary and key. You're in number eight, a nice secluded little hideaway with a beautiful view of the lake. It's also got a pier, should you decide you'd like to swim or fish." She leaned forward and pointed to a laminated map attached to her desk. "You'll find a map of the property in your packet as well, but things are clearly marked so you shouldn't have any problems. We'll have an informal meet and greet in the lodge at six. It isn't mandatory, but we urge you to come. In the meantime—"

Jamie sensed movement behind him and watched Tewanda's warm brown gaze turn frosty. He glanced over his shoulder and saw a man strolling toward them across the room.

"Where's Audrey?" the guy asked, interrupting them rudely. Jamie scowled.

Though he knew it was ridiculous, he instantly disliked the guy.

"I'm with a guest right now, Derrick," Tewanda said coolly. "As I was saying Mr. Flanagan, settle in and—"

"I can see that," Derrick interrupted again. He shot Jamie a condescending look, one that somehow managed to be pitying and patronizing at once. It was a "you-poor-weak-bastard" look, which made Jamie's blood pressure rise and his right fist involuntarily clench.

"But I'm in a bit of a hurry and I need to see Audrey before I go." He paused. "She hasn't returned any of my calls, which can only lead me to assume that you haven't passed along any of my messages."

Tewanda's nose flared as she drew in a breath. "Oh, I've passed them along, all right. Maybe she just doesn't want to talk to you."

He smiled as if the idea was out of the question. "Oh, I doubt that. Page her," he ordered. "I'm pressed for time."

With a tight "excuse me" and a murderous look, Tewanda lifted a walkie-talkie from the desk.

The man leaned over to Jamie, as though he were an ally. "Good help's hard to find these days," he said, shooting a look at Tewanda. "I've tried to tell Audrey that she should let her go, but does she listen to me?"

He certainly hoped not, Jamie thought, sidling away from him. What a prick.

"Audrey, Derrick is here disrupting a check-in and won't leave until he speaks with you. Could you come up here and get rid of him— Er, I mean *talk* to him, please?" she asked with faux sweetness.

"See," Derrick said. "Such impertinence. If I ever have any say-so—and I will," he added with a confident smile, "—then she'll be the first of many changes I make around here."

Tewanda merely rolled her eyes. "Oh, don't worry, Derrick. The day you have any say-so will be the day I quit."

"Where's she at?" he asked, ignoring her comment. He checked his watch again and glanced impatiently toward the door.

"I don't have her on GPS," she snapped. "How the hell should I know?"

A startled laugh clogged Jamie's throat and he and Tewanda shared a smile. "Sorry," she mumbled.

"It's all right," he told her, waving it off.

"What are you apologizing to him for?" Derrick asked, seemingly offended. "It's me you were rude to."

She tidied a stack of papers on her desk and grunted. "In a perfect world, you wouldn't exist."

Jamie had only been in the man's company for a total of thirty seconds and found that he wholeheartedly concurred.

Derrick scowled and readied his mouth for a comeback, but before he could utter a sound, the woman from the photo on Garrett's desk walked in.

Sonofabitch, Jamie thought, his suspicions confirmed. Oh, this was not good. Not good at all.

As an elite graduate of Ranger School, Jamie had been trained to notice every detail. For instance, the minute he'd walked into this room, he'd noted everything from the exits—doors and windows—to the half-eaten jelly doughnut hidden behind a potted plant on the desk. In a pinch he could describe the pile of the carpet, the picture hanging on the opposite wall and could cite the programs currently running on the computer. It was this very training that enabled him to quickly catalogue Audrey Kincaid's every feature.

In the time it took her to cross the room, Jamie had noted that her hair wasn't black as it had seemed in the picture, but rather a very dark brown just a degree shy of black. Espresso, he decided. Her eyes were the same, a clear intelligent blue that shimmered with wit and warmth. She was petite—five-four or under, he imagined—but with an athletic build that was surprisingly curvy. She had a small mole just up and to the right of her lush mouth and when she smiled, an adorable dimple winked in her left cheek. She was sexy and enchanting and delicious and he found himself fighting the inexplicable urge to lick her all over.

Which wouldn't be good because she was totally off-limits. Garrett would kill him. After he cut his pride and joy off and force-fed it to him, Jamie reminded himself grimly.

He'd do well to remember that.

"Derrick," she said in a softly chiding voice. "I thought you'd be on your way to the airport by now."

Derrick grinned, gathered her into an awkward hug and said, "I couldn't leave without giving you a proper goodbye." He nuzzled her cheek and, though it could have only been wishful thinking on Jamie's part, she winced as if she didn't particularly care for his attention. Looking ready to retch, Tewanda rolled her eyes.

"You didn't have to do that," she said, disentangling herself from him. "You, uh... You don't want to miss your flight."

"No, no, of course not. I just wanted to give you a reason to miss me."

Audrey smiled, rather weakly, it seemed, but didn't say anything.

He ran a finger down her nose. "And I also wanted to remind you to think about what I'd asked you."

This time she chuckled, but there was almost a sick-sounding quality to it that Jamie was certain both he and Tewanda had heard, but that had completely gone unnoticed by Derrick. In fact, he got the distinct impression that Derrick missed a lot.

"Er...no worries," she told him. "I'm not likely to forget."

"I guess not," he said, smiling smugly. "All right then. I'd better be off." He bent down and kissed her on the cheek. "I'll see you Sunday...and I'll expect an answer," he added ominously. Without so much as a backward glance to the rest of the occupants in the room, he strode out.

"Want me to give him an answer?" Tewanda offered hopefully when the door closed behind Derrick.

Audrey's shoulders sagged with a sigh of obvious relief. "No," she told her. "That won't be necessary." She pushed a hand through her hair, then looked up and for the first time her gaze landed on Jamie. "Oh," she said, her eyes widening in obvious embarrassment.

Tewanda grinned. "This is our newest guest—Jamie Flanagan," she said. "The Colonel's friend," she added significantly.

Impossibly, her eyes widened further, then another "oh" slipped from between her lips. Three beats passed, then she gave her head a small shake. She smiled and hurried forward to offer her hand.

Against his better judgment he took it and, to his immediate chagrin, his palm tingled where it touched hers. Heat detonated in his loins and a curious warmth expanded in his chest.

Now that was novel, Jamie thought, somewhat startled by the singularly disturbing reaction. His dick had stirred the instant he'd seen her—no surprise there because it nodded at almost every woman of the right age with a halfway decent rack—but this was the first time he'd ever gotten a charge out of merely touching a woman's hand. While the picture of her might have been compelling, seeing her in the flesh was nothing short of magnetic. Jamie gritted his teeth as more prophet-of-doom musings rolled through his head.

"It's a pleasure, Mr. Flanagan."

"Jamie, please," he told her, smiling, as a litany of curses reeled through his head.

"Jamie, then. I'm Audrey. Welcome to Unwind."

Hell more like, Jamie thought, because guarding this woman without seducing her was going to be an exercise in restraint which would result in the most perverse sort of torture he could imagine.

Unwind hell.

He'd be lucky if he didn't come un-glued, un-hinged, un-wound, or un-manned by the time this week was over.

"SINCE MR. FLANAGAN IS a special guest, why don't you show him to his cottage personally?" Tewanda suggested sweetly.

Unable to tear her gaze away from the man in question, it took Audrey a few seconds to respond. "Er…sure. I'd be happy to. If you'll just come with me," she said trying to sound more professional than the half-wit she'd undoubtedly just appeared to be.

Sheesh, Audrey thought, resisting the pressing urge to fan herself as they walked outside into the cool autumn air. You'd think she'd never seen a good-looking man before.

But this man wasn't merely good-looking she thought with a covert peek from the corner of her eye—he was *pure* take-your-breath-away nipple-tingling flash-fire-across-the-thighs *eye candy*.

This was her grandfather's friend? *This* was the guy who needed special attention?

Quite frankly, she couldn't imagine that he didn't get all the attention that he wanted.

Of the female variety, at least, she thought with a quirk of her lips.

He had that look, that cocked, locked, ready to rock sexuality that instantly put a woman in mind of warm massage oil and thigh-quaking orgasms.

Unfortunately, to her immeasurable chagrin considering she'd only been in his presence a mere sixty seconds, that included herself.

That certainly didn't bode well for a week of what her grandfather had insisted should be intense one-on-one attention. Particularly as she was supposed to be considering a marriage proposal. But that was a whole other problem she'd simply have to think about later, she decided, channeling a little Scarlet O'Hara.

Right now, she was finding it hard enough to regulate her breathing, much less anything else. She was too distracted by the disturbingly masculine line of his jaw, those sleepy hazel eyes which managed to be both wise and wicked and that shock of adorably curly brown hair.

He was clearly an alpha—from the jut of that

jaw to the swagger in his step, everything about him screamed *merited* confidence—but that hair softened him up, made him approachable and gave him a beta boy-next-door quality that mysteriously added to his overall sex appeal. Audrey felt a smile tug at her lips. No doubt he could make an orchid bloom in an arctic winter or charm the habit right off a nun if the mood struck…then convince her it was her idea.

And she'd bet he didn't scream like a girl when he came, either.

Mercy.

Jamie paused next to what was clearly a rental sedan. "Do I drive up to the cottage?" he asked.

Audrey shook her head and indicated an area to the side of the office. "Up there will be fine. If you'd like to leave your bags with me, I'll wait here while you park."

"Bag."

"I'm sorry?"

"You said 'bags.'" An interesting display of muscle action rippled across his back as he reached into the back seat, pulled out a small duffel and, wearing a lazy smile, handed it to her. "It's bag. Singular."

Audrey chewed the corner of her lip, eying the

duffel skeptically. "You have almost a week's worth of clothes in *this* bag?"

"With a couple of changes to spare."

She chuckled and inclined her head. He certainly had the art of packing light down to a science. Of course, given his military training she supposed that was habit as much as necessity. The more they packed, the more they had to carry. Too bad that some of the other people who came here didn't have that same mentality. If they had to schlep their weighty Louis Vuitton everywhere themselves, they might rethink packing everything but the kitchen sink.

Feeling herself intrigued beyond what she knew to be prudent, Audrey waited while Jamie moved the car. He made quick work of it, locked up, then loped with easy grace back down to where she stood and took the bag. "All right, then," he said, casually taking in their surroundings. "Where to?"

Audrey set off and pointed toward the lake. "Right down there."

"This is a beautiful place," Jamie remarked, seemingly enjoying the fall landscape. Tall trees dressed in their finest foliage soared overhead and painted a mirror image on the lake's rippling surface. New England asters bloomed in a purple perfusion of color along the various winding stone paths throughout camp and a couple of bickering squirrels squabbled over acorns. Stark white steep-roofed cottages were tucked along the lake and deep into the tree line, giving the impression of an old Colonial village.

"Thanks," she said. "I'm proud of it. It was in pretty bad shape when I first bought it. Beautiful land, of course." She slid him a glance. "It's not called Lake Bliss for nothing. But the buildings and landscaping were all in need of serious repair."

"How long have you been in business?"

"This is our fourth season."

"Season?"

"We don't operate year-round," she explained. "The winters are too intense and frankly, we don't have enough business to merit being open beyond Christmas. We run camps March through November."

Jamie nodded. "So what do you do those other months? Hunker down here?" He glanced around. "I'm assuming you live on site."

"I do," Audrey confirmed with a smile. She gestured toward her own place, a slightly larger variation of the guest cottages. "I usually spend a month recuperating, a month vegging out and another month traveling and visiting family. In February, we're gearing up toward a new season, so even though we aren't technically open, we're here getting things in order."

He smiled and she felt that grin all the way down to her little toes. "Sounds like you've got things down to a science."

Audrey chuckled, shoving her hair away from her face. "Not really," she said. "But we've found a system that seems to be working for us." She mounted the steps to his cottage. "Ah. Here we are."

Jamie inserted the key into the lock and let himself in.

"It's fully stocked," Audrey told him, stepping in behind him. Which was quite nice because she got a wonderful view of his delectable ass—the ass she was not supposed to be noticing. She grimaced. Somehow she imagined this was not the sort of *special attention* her grandfather had in mind. "Linens, pantry—everything. Naturally, we've met any special requests which were on your application form, but if you've forgotten anything, there's a general store just up the hill. If you can't find what you need there, let us know and we'll take care of it. No worries. That's our motto."

Jamie dropped his bag into a recliner. "Special requests?" A line wrinkled his forehead. "I didn't make any special requests."

Audrey forcibly flattened a smile and cleared her throat. "Er…my grandfather made several on your behalf."

"I'll just bet he did," Jamie muttered darkly with a comical grimace.

"You'll find Guinness beer in the fridge and Jameson whiskey in the cabinet." She cocked her head. "Tribute to your Irish heritage, I presume?"

Jamie nodded and grinned. "It's the best."

Audrey'd had Guinness before, but had never been much of a whiskey drinker. She confessed as much. "It's too much," she said. "I don't care for the burn."

"*Uisce beatha.*" He sighed, absently scratching his chest.

"Come again?"

"*Uisce beatha.* It's Gaelic for 'water of life.'"

"Oh."

He chuckled. "Trust me, the Irish know how to make a good whiskey. You'll have to try it. It's smoother. It's got a sweet honey flavor and slides like silk down your throat."

Audrey resisted the pressing urge to fidget and let go a small uneven breath. Well, when he put it like that, who wouldn't want to drink it?

Jamie crossed his arms over his chest and leaned a heavily muscled shoulder against the wall. His too-sexy lips quirked with droll humor. "What other special requests did the Colonel make for me?"

"Oh, just a few things," Audrey told him lightly. "Books, medications. The usual."

Liar, liar pants on fire. There'd been nothing *usual* about the things her grandfather had specifically asked for on Jamie's behalf. And in fact, now that she'd met him, she couldn't imagine that he'd need any of them.

Jamie frowned. "Books? Med—?"

"Anyway," Audrey smoothly interrupted before they could get into any of that. She moved toward the door, preparing to make a swift exit. "You'll want to get settled, I'm sure. Take your time, but do be sure and come up to the lodge at six. It's informal, but we like to go over everything that Unwind has to offer. I'll be taking care of you personally this week."

"Personally, eh?" he asked with a grin that would ignite water.

Audrey blushed. "That's right." She cleared her throat. "Anyway, be sure and bring your schedule—"

"Schedule?"

"Yes. It's in there—" she gestured toward the manila envelope on top of his bag "—and we'll get you on the road to relaxation."

He muttered something else she didn't quite understand.

"I'm sorry?"

"It was nothing," Jamie said quickly, offering her a smile she knew he'd conjured solely for her benefit. It might have been false, but it was still potent. At any rate, he clearly didn't want to be here and, as her grandfather had said, was only acting on the Colonel's orders. That was going to make things much more difficult, Audrey thought, but she'd promised her grandfather that she'd do her best to take care of him.

For the next week, this guy was hers—the mere thought made her insides quiver—and even with the wacky trumped up so-called hobbies her grandfather had supplied for Jamie, she fully expected to enjoy herself much more than she should.

4

YOU CAN GO ON—Dealing with Erectile Dysfunction.

Coping with Incontinence.

Jamie snorted and tossed the books aside, then pulled his cell from the clip at his waist and dialed Garrett directly. "What?" he asked when the Colonel answered the phone. "Was *Chicken Soup for the Psychopath's Soul* on backorder?"

Garrett chuckled, the twisted bastard. "I see you've arrived."

"I have."

"And everything's in order?"

"Everything but your sense of humor. Basket-weaving? Watercolors? Ballroom dancing? Just exactly when were you planning to have me guard her?" Jamie asked, completely exasperated. Hobbies, hell. "Because the *relaxing* schedule I'm looking at leaves very little time for that."

"Tsk, tsk," said the Colonel. "You make it sound like you're not going to have a good time."

Jamie moved his duffel out of the recliner and dropped heavily into it. He flicked a casual glance around the living room and deemed it to his liking. Comfortable furniture, natural gender-neutral decor. A nice view of the lake. Not bad at all. "I didn't think the purpose of this mission was to ensure that I had a good time. I thought I was here to protect Audrey."

"Ah, Audrey, is it?"

Jamie felt his fingers tighten around the cordless phone. "That's her name. You didn't expect me to call her Ms. Kincaid, did you?"

"No, and I don't want anyone calling her Mrs. Derrick Willis either, which is the real reason you are there. Take notes. You're about to receive orders."

Jamie blinked, stunned. "What? I thought you said you wanted me to protect her from a personal enemy."

"I do—that enemy is Derrick Willis."

Jamie leaned forward in his chair. *Derrick? How could Derrick be his personal enemy? What the fu—*

"I have it on good authority that he's asked my granddaughter to marry him and has given her until the end of the week to make up her mind," Garrett said.

Jamie stilled. So *that* was the question Derrick-the-ass had been referring to, Jamie realized, suddenly sickened. Though he'd barely had time to rub two thoughts together since he'd gotten here, he had to admit that Audrey choosing a boyfriend like that sonofabitch was a little disheartening. Quite frankly, he would have thought she'd had better taste.

What was the draw? he wondered. It damned sure wasn't personality or sex appeal. The guy was provokingly abrasive at best and Jamie had personally seen her cringe when Derrick had tried to hug her. That certainly wouldn't make a happy marriage. It didn't make any sense.

And he sure as hell didn't see how he was supposed to "protect" her from Derrick.

"I don't understand," Jamie told him, thoroughly confused. "Derrick's not even here."

"I know. He's on a business trip."

What? Jamie wondered. Did he have the place bugged? "How did you know th—"

"Suffice it to say I have an excellent source in place who also has my granddaughter's best interests at heart."

Ah. *Tewanda.*

He was beginning to get the picture—albeit a vastly different one to what had originally been painted—but he still didn't see how he figured in it. "Sir, with all due respect, I fail to see how I can—"

Garrett chuckled. "For someone with a genius-level IQ, you certainly aren't doing a bang-up job of putting things together, Flanagan."

He supposed not, Jamie thought, completely baffled. He couldn't hit a target that wasn't here. What the hell did Garrett want him to do? Follow Derrick? If so, then why had he arranged for Jamie to be in place here? It didn't make any sense. Exactly what did the Colonel have in mind—

"Oh, for heaven's sake," Garrett finally snapped. "You're bait."

If Jamie hadn't had a death grip on the phone he would have dropped it. He felt his eyes widen and his jaw drop. "I'm *what?*"

"Bait," Garrett repeated calmly. "Your reputation with the ladies makes you the perfect man for this mission, Flanagan. Oh, I suppose McCann or Payne would have done okay as well, but in order to make absolutely sure that Audrey doesn't permanently attach herself to that pompous moron, I thought I'd err on the side of caution and send you in."

Silence stretched across the line while Jamie tried to process what the Colonel had just told him.

"You see," Garrett continued, "if my granddaughter is even remotely attracted to you, she wouldn't dream of saying 'I do' to that gelled-up windbag. She has too much class. And it's no secret that you have a certain talent with women... So here are your orders and you'd better heed them to the letter," Garrett warned. "Otherwise, I assure you that you'll be very, *very* sorry." He paused, letting the threat sink in. "For the next five days I want you to shadow my granddaughter. Spend time with her, flirt with her, compliment her. Do whatever it is that you do to get women to fall all over you. But that is all. I'm not pimping you out to my granddaughter, Flanagan," he said gruffly, some of that legendary piss and gravel in his voice. "Baseball's an all-American game, so I'll put it into terms I'm sure you'll understand. You are on-deck, but you will never get to bat, do you understand?"

Still in a state of shock, Jamie cleared his throat. "Yes, sir."

"First base is forbidden. Second base is forbidden. Third base is forbidden. If you get anywhere near home plate, you'll *need* that book on erectile dysfunction. You'll also need a surgeon to remove my foot from your ass. Is there any part of this that's unclear?"

"No, sir."

"This is a pseudo-seduction, for lack of a better description. I don't want her to want *you*, per se. I just want her to want anyone but Derrick. You're there to instill doubt and I know you can make that happen."

He could, Jamie knew. He just didn't want to do it. Not to her. It was wrong and underhanded, a personal interference he knew that she wouldn't appreciate. "Sir, I realize that I don't know your granddaughter, but if she ever finds out that you've done something like this, she'll—"

"That's why she'll never find out," Garrett said in his typical omnipotent voice. "She's special," he told Jamie. "She deserves someone who will see that. That blowhard Derrick sees nothing beyond himself."

Jamie passed a hand over his face. "Yeah," he admitted. "I noticed."

"You met him?" he asked, surprised.

"He interrupted my check-in. He came in and demanded to see Audrey."

"Then certainly you can see why I've resorted to these somewhat…unorthodox measures."

Actually, though Jamie didn't appreciate being the means to which Garrett reached his end, he did see why the Colonel would take such a drastic approach to derailing the relationship. He couldn't imagine any woman being permanently interested in Derrick, much less Audrey. Why? he wondered, intrigued beyond what was appropriate. What was she doing with someone who was so obviously wrong for her?

Jamie's head began to hurt. "If I'm going to do this, then I need a little back story."

"There's no *if*, Flanagan," Garrett told him gruffly. "You owe me and you agreed to my terms."

And there it was, Jamie thought with a mental sigh. "Fine. Bring me up to speed. How long have they been dating?"

"Too long."

Anything beyond a minute would be too long, but that wasn't the answer he'd been looking for. "Naturally. Could you be a little more specific?"

"A little more than a year and half."

So definitely long enough to know whether they wanted to take things to the next level. Clearly Derrick did, otherwise he wouldn't have issued an ultimatum. And it had to have been an ultimatum, otherwise he wouldn't have added a time frame into the mix. So what were the consequences of saying no? Jamie wondered. A breakup? Most likely. Derrick seemed like the type.

"Is Audrey aware of the fact that you don't approve of Derrick?" Jamie knew the answer to that question before it was even fully out of his mouth. The Colonel was always willing to share his opinion—whether a person wanted to hear it or not.

The Colonel laughed. "What do you think?"

"Right," Jamie said, feeling like an idiot. "And yet she's still seeing him. Why's she bucking you on this? What's so special about Derrick?"

"I don't think there's anything special about Derrick."

"You don't, but she obviously does. Surely she's given you an explanation as to why she's still with him."

The Colonel hesitated. "She has," he conceded. "But I'm not sure I should share her personal business with you."

A bark of laughter erupted from Jamie's throat. Oh, now this was rich. "You've got to be kidding me. You've sent me up here to practically seduce her away from this other guy and yet your conscience is giving you a problem with *this?*" He chuckled darkly. "You need to check your moral compass."

"*Practically* is the key word there, Flanagan," Garrett growled. "But—" he sighed "—I suppose you're right. The more information you have, the better armed you'll be to deal with the situation."

Exactly, Jamie thought. Besides, he was genuinely curious. What on earth would make a great girl like Audrey interested in someone as self-absorbed and shallow as Derrick?

"My granddaughter is a very caring person, Flanagan—unusually empathetic—and as such, has always had a habit of attracting people, most often men, who require a lot of her. So much of her, in fact, that she found herself emotionally bankrupt. And sick. Derrick's appeal is that he's not like that. He's arrogant, but not damaged. At least, that's what I got out of what she's shared with me," the Colonel said, his voice ringing with a hell-if-I-know sort of resignation. He blew out a breath. "Anyway, I don't blame her for wanting someone who doesn't suck the life out of her, but I think she's swung too far in the other direction. She needs to find a happy medium. If she marries Derrick, that'll never happen."

It took Jamie a few seconds to absorb and digest what Garrett had just shared. "So, in other words, Derrick's easy."

"That too," Garrett replied. "You have your orders, Flanagan. I'll call for updates." He disconnected.

Jamie turned the phone off, leaned back into the recliner and let out a breath. Ten seconds later he turned the phone back on and dialed Ranger Security.

"You aren't going to believe this shit," he said in way of greeting when Payne answered his direct line. Jamie briefed his friend on recent events and waited while Payne took it all in.

"Let me get this straight. The boyfriend is the personal threat and he's sent you in there to 'pseudo-seduce' her away from him?"

"In a nutshell, yes."

To Jamie's extreme annoyance, Payne laughed. Not just a small series of chuckles, but a gut-rolling guffaw that set Jamie's nerves on edge. "That's c-cracked, man. I feel for you."

"Yeah, it really sounds like it," Jamie griped.

"Look at it this way. It's not dangerous, right?"

If he kept his pecker in his pants, no, Jamie thought. But if he snapped and ended up giving her a real seduction, then mortal danger was almost certain. Garrett would most definitely kill him.

"Not in the traditional sense, no."

Payne paused, evidently reading the ambiguity in that statement. "Damn. She's pretty, isn't she?"

Pretty didn't begin to cover it. She was beautiful in every sense of the word. Jamie had noted those soul-soothing eyes in the photograph in Garrett's office, but actually looking into them and feeling that calming sensation in her presence was quite…disconcerting. Garrett's explanation as to why she was with Derrick made perfect sense. He could easily see a needy person sucking up her goodness like a greedy parasite attached to her soul.

She wasn't seeing Derrick because she was in love with him—it was an act of self-preservation.

But Garrett was right. There had to be a happy medium. Derrick might not be draining her at the moment, but eventually her own unhappiness and dissatisfaction with the relationship would do the very thing she was trying to avoid.

Though he didn't approve of how the Colonel had chosen to interfere—and the part he'd ultimately be playing in it—he had to admit that he could see where she'd be better off.

She needed protecting all right. She needed protection from herself.

The question was…who was going to protect him?

When he'd thought he was just supposed to guard her, he'd worried about keeping his hands to himself. He'd known that it was going to take a Herculean effort on his part to try and keep his distance. Now he was charged with the task of wooing her…with no reward. What sort of divinely twisted infernal hell was this? Jamie wondered. To seduce with no seduction?

To seduce *her,* of all people?

"Yeah, she's pretty," Jamie finally confirmed.

And he was screwed.

5

Atlanta

PAYNE TOOK A PULL from his beer, then finished bringing Guy up to speed on Jamie's current situation. He laughed. "Can you believe that shit?"

Looking just as mystified as he undoubtedly had when Jamie had told him the nature of Garrett's "favor," Guy shook his head and smiled faintly. "You know, I fully expected him to utilize our skills, but that was one of Jamie's I would have never dreamed Garrett would risk putting into use. Especially with his own granddaughter."

"He's got a helluva lot more trust in our friend than I do," Payne admitted. "He said she's pretty."

Guy winced. "Damn."

"I know."

"I smell trouble."

He did, too. It was like turning a bloodhound

loose, then telling him not to follow the trail. Furthermore, he'd heard a bit of I'm-screwed misery in Jamie's voice that definitely didn't get his vote of confidence. Garrett undoubtedly was banking on Jamie's ability to take an order—or take one for the team—but this was different.

Jamie wasn't a Ranger anymore.

He was still a man of his word, but more than one man had broken a promise when it came to a woman. Sex did something to a guy. Made him weak in a way that nothing else could. Payne's lips quirked. Hell, his father was a perfect example of that.

Which was why he'd never be.

Guy shot him a considering look. "Makes me wonder what he's got in store for us."

Him, too. Payne had been certain that Garrett had planned to use them for Uncle Sam. He'd never dreamed that the crafty old bastard had planned on cashing in those favors for himself. Point of fact, it shed a completely different light on things. He paused, tracing a bead of moisture down the side of his beer, and re-evaluating. Not that it would have changed anything—they would have agreed to his terms anyway. They'd wanted out at any cost. Still…

"I know," he finally said. His lips curled into a grim smile. "Let's just hope like hell he doesn't have any more relatives in need of rescue."

"Oh, I don't think we have to worry about that," Guy said. A smile rolled around his lips and a bark of dry laughter erupted from his throat. "Evidently you and I aren't sexy enough."

Payne chuckled. "Speak for yourself, you ugly bastard. He didn't send me because he was afraid she'd fall in love with me. I was *too* much man."

Guy smiled, grabbing his beer. "Go to hell."

Yeah, and he could tell Jamie hello when he got there. He had a grim suspicion his buddy had been sent straight into the bowels of darkness.

"SO THAT'S A BRIEF OVERVIEW of what we do here at Unwind. Any questions?" Audrey glanced around the room, waited a couple of beats, then smiled. "Okay then. Remember…no worries."

Though she'd been trying not to stare at Jamie, her gaze kept inexplicably wandering over to where he stood in the back of the room. Even if she hadn't known he had a special forces military background, she would have recognized the signs.

Casual, but alert, he constantly scanned the

room, observing. She'd watched him note the exits, the number of people present and his demeanor seemed to suggest he could be a protector or predator, whichever the case may be. For reasons which made her question her own sanity, she found that wholly thrilling. In fact, she could honestly say that she'd never had such an overwhelming reaction to a man before.

"God, that man is beautiful."

Audrey barely refrained from jumping. Damn Tewanda. "Don't sneak up on me like that," she chided, tearing her gaze away from the beautiful man in question.

"If you hadn't been staring so hard at him, you would have seen me walk up."

Since she couldn't argue with that, she decided to change the subject. "So, what do you think about this group?"

Tewanda nodded. "Seems good." She inclined her head toward a tall balding man in the corner. "He's a crier. We'll need to watch him." Next she turned her attention to a petite blonde with blood-red nails who carried a Prada knockoff. "That one. She's going to be a problem. She's already called three times about things that she says are 'wrong' and aren't her preferences. But don't worry I have everything on file and you know I don't make mistakes like that."

No, she didn't. Given their satisfaction guarantee promise, Tewanda was neurotically meticulous about the details. In fact, in their four years in business, she'd never made a mistake. Needless to say, she was an invaluable asset to Unwind and to Audrey, in particular. She also had the uncanny ability to size people up. Tewanda could spot a potential problem guest with almost psychic accuracy.

Audrey nodded, accepting her assessment. "Anybody else?"

"Yeah, there's one more."

"Point 'em out," she said from the corner of her mouth, smiling warmly at passersby.

"No need," she said. "Here he comes."

"What? Who?"

"Him," she said significantly as Jamie sidled through the crowd toward them.

"Jamie?" Audrey said, startled. "What makes you say a thing like that?" Had she missed something? she wondered. Granted she'd initially been too preoccupied by the rest of him to note the sadness lingering around and in those mesmerizing hazel eyes, but she'd glimpsed it tonight.

Big time.

"Don't you play dumb with me," Tewanda told her, chuckling under her breath. "I know you think he's hot. You want him."

"Tewanda."

"Tewanda, Tewanda," she mimicked, as though she got tired of hearing her name repeated in that exasperated tone. "You know I'm right. That boy isn't just going to be trouble. He *is* trouble. Especially for you."

"Why for me?" she asked, instinctively knowing her friend was right.

"Haven't you been listening to me? Because you want him," she said with the sort of exaggerated patience used to communicate something to a person who might be a little slow.

"I just met him," Audrey chided with a nervous eye roll, an almost, but not outright denial.

"Doesn't matter. It's the animal instinct, honey. And I predict that you two will be going at it like a couple of Viagra-crazed rabbits by the end of the week."

Before she could shape her lips to refute that outlandish comment, a vision of her and Jamie, tangled up and sweaty and doing precisely what Tewanda had suggested materialized in her mind's eye, making her momentarily breathless. Her nipples beaded behind her bra, her knees weakened and a melting tingle started low in her belly and settled in her sex.

Oh, sweet Jesus.

If thinking about making it with him did this to her, then she couldn't begin to imagine what being with him would really be like.

Actually, that wasn't true.

She *could* imagine, and the resulting vision had an almost virtual reality effect. In fact, if she didn't derail this line of thinking immediately, she was going to have an immaculate orgasm. Right here in the lodge, amid a roomful of people. Audrey released a shuddering breath.

Now that was some potent sex appeal.

He sidled over and smiled, unwittingly upping her heart rate. Then her gaze tangled with his and, in the nanosecond before he could put a guard firmly in place, Audrey glimpsed a pain so intense she felt it deep in her belly. Oh, sweet Lord, she thought, as nausea threatened and her vision blackened around the edges. She *had* missed something.

A huge something.

Stark pain, grief, regret—they were all there, a

perfect cocktail of misery. Her grandfather had been right, Audrey thought, swallowing. Jamie Flanagan had one helluva demon shadowing him. He disguised it well beneath effortless sex appeal and lazy charm, but she saw it, and more importantly felt it. In fact, while she'd had vast experience in feeling other people's pain, she could honestly say that she'd never suffered from this sort of intensity.

"Ladies," he said, jerking Audrey from her disquieting reverie.

Tewanda grinned. "Are you ready to unwind?" she asked him. "You look a little tense."

"I'm fine, thanks," Jamie told her, eyes twinkling.

"Audrey's a licensed masseuse," Tewanda said, much to Audrey's annoyance. Still a bit shaken, she resisted the urge to pinch her friend.

Audrey summoned a tight smile. "True, however we have a regular masseuse on staff. Part of the luxury of an expanding clientele." She managed a chuckle.

"So you don't have to be so *hands-on,* then," Jamie said, obviously enjoying her discomfort.

"Right."

"But since Jamie here is a *special* guest of the

Colonel and you're supposed to be taking care of him personally, surely you wouldn't mind working out a few of his kinks, right, Audrey?"

Did Maine have the death penalty? Audrey wondered, sending her friend a murderously sweet smile. "Not at all," she said in what she knew was far from a normal voice.

Looking entirely too pleased with herself, Tewanda leaned forward as though she was about to impart a kernel of significant advice. "In fact, I can't think of a better way to start your Unwind experience than with a relaxing massage." She bobbed her head in a brisk nod. "I have one every week."

Jamie's eyes twinkled with humor. "Really?"

"Oh, yes." She preened. "It does wonders for my complexion."

"I've never had one. At least from a professional, that is," he amended.

And on that singularly disturbing note, Audrey cleared her throat. "You know what I think is the best way to start your Unwind experience?" she asked Jamie. "With a nice session of water colors down by the lake. My grandfather says you're quite the artist."

A soft chuckle erupted from his throat. "Really? I didn't realize he was a fan of my work. I'll have to paint something *special* for him."

Actually, her grandfather had said no such thing and she fully suspected that Jamie hadn't painted any sort of picture, much less a watercolor, since primary school. Playing along, was he? Now that was interesting. And it would be fun, considering her grandfather had already explained his bizarre preferences and hobby choices for Jamie. With the exception of the whiskey and beer, the *preferences* had been jokes. As for the hobby choices, her grandfather had chosen them so that Jamie could learn certain virtues. Like patience.

Audrey grinned. "Oh, good. We can have it framed in town and ship it to him before you leave."

His eyes glinted with knowing humor. "Excellent."

Marginally relaxing, Audrey rocked back a little on her heels.

"But I'll still want that massage."

And every muscle atrophied again, particularly the ones in her face which controlled her smile. "Of course," she said because she couldn't think of any other response. Dissembling while visions of her hands on his warm, naked skin, kneading those impressive muscles was completely beyond her. Audrey released a silent quivering sigh.

Time to go home, she decided. "Well, if you don't have any more questions, I think I'm going to call it an evening."

"I'll go with you," Tewanda said. She did an admirable job of looking concerned. "I don't like you walking up that hill all alone."

Honestly, this was over the top, even for Tewanda. Exasperated, Audrey shook her head. "I have walked up that hill alone every night of every season since we opened, Tewanda," she told her through partially gritted teeth. "I think I can manage."

"That may be true but—"

"Tewanda."

"I'll walk you home," Jamie offered, playing right into her maniacal matchmaking friend's hands.

"Really," Audrey insisted. "It isn't necessary."

"But it'll relax me," he said with a half-smile that made her belly do an odd little jump.

Oh, well…how nice for him. She wished she could say the same for herself.

"BE SURE TO GIVE MY REGARDS to the Colonel," Jamie leaned in and whispered to Tewanda before following a somewhat irate Audrey out of the room.

"Sure thing, Ace," Tewanda told him. She grinned and twinkled her fingers at him as he walked away. She was clearly enjoying herself, Jamie thought, fighting a chuckle. No doubt she'd received her instructions from the Colonel as well and was taking her role as matchmaker quite seriously.

While it was easy to laugh at her machinations, Jamie knew better than to discount them. As Audrey's right-hand man, so to speak, and clearly a good friend, she was better positioned than anybody to know what was happening with Audrey. If she was trying this hard to make sure that Audrey didn't marry Derrick, she had to have good reason.

Which made the Colonel sending him in as he had all the more understandable.

Sure, Jamie didn't like it, and no doubt being with her without *being with her* was going to be sheer hell, but she had two very discerning people covertly interfering on her behalf—three, if he counted himself, which, for reasons he didn't un-derstand, he wasn't prepared to do just yet—and that told him enough about what he was doing to make him feel marginally better about his role in the deception.

Besides, he didn't have any choice. He'd owed Garrett.

Jamie opened the door for her, ushering Audrey out into the cool autumn air. Dusk had come and gone, bringing darkness and a spattering of bright stars. Fluffy clouds glowed in the moonlight and drifted lazily across the deep navy sky.

"She's a piece of work, isn't she?" Jamie remarked lightly as they descended the steps onto the walk.

Audrey chuckled, the sound soft, soothing and feminine against his ears. "Tewanda? That's one way of describing her." She crossed her arms over her chest, huddling further into her jacket. "I'm thinking 'fired' would be another."

Jamie laughed. "Surely not?"

"Nah," she relented. "I couldn't do what I do without her. She's invaluable—and insufferable. That's part of her charm."

"Look at it this way," Jamie told her. "I bet you never have to wonder what she thinks."

She shot him a pointedly wry look. "Much like my grandfather."

Jamie tilted his head back as another laugh rumbled up his throat. "I definitely wouldn't argue with that assessment."

"He strong-armed you into coming here, didn't he?"

That was one way of putting it, Jamie thought. "In a manner of speaking."

"In a manner of speaking? He filled out all of your paperwork, sent your itinerary and told you when to be here."

"What tipped you off?" Jamie teased. "The book on erectile dysfunction, the bottle of Metamucil or the package of adult diapers in the bathroom?"

"What?" she deadpanned with wide-eyed innocence. "You mean you aren't an impotent, incontinent bed wetter?"

Smiling, Jamie ducked his head toward his chest and shoved his hands into his front pockets. "Er…that would be a big fat negative."

"I asked him about all of that. He was only joking with those things, you know," she said. "Wanted to prep you to relax with a good laugh."

He figured she'd asked about Jamie's so-called "preferences", Jamie thought. He would have. He had to give the old guy a hand, though—he was quick on his feet. "I know," Jamie said. "He's always good for a laugh." Jamie scratched his head, pretended to be confused. "Did he happen to mention why he listed my hobbies as basket-weaving, watercolors and ballroom dancing?"

Audrey shot him a smile. "Ah…those are 're-laxing' things he thinks you ought to try. Basket-weaving requires patience, watercolor skill, and every man needs to know how to dance. Or so sayeth the Colonel."

So he'd conjured an answer for everything, then. Jamie shook his head. Somehow he wasn't surprised. "And we, er… We have to adhere to that schedule while I'm here?"

Audrey turned onto the sidewalk which led up to her house. Her porch light glowed in the distance, illuminating potted plants—mums, mostly—and white wicker outdoor furniture out-fitted with comfy cushions.

"We don't have to," she said. "The purpose of Unwind is to enable you to relax, but—" She hes-itated, nervously chewed her bottom lip. "I was told to personally keep you on task and to 'expect resistance.'"

She mounted the steps to her front door and turned to face him. The wind toyed with the ends of her hair, sending a long lock against her neck. He was suddenly hit with the urge to wind that wayward lock around his finger and draw her to him. "For obvious reasons, it would make my life a lot easier if you'd simply give them a try."

Check and checkmate, Jamie thought, realizing that he should simply bow to the master and accept defeat. The Colonel had thought of every-thing. How could he look into those calmly pleading gorgeous blue eyes and say no?

Did he want to basket weave? Er…no.

Did he think he'd enjoy painting? That was a bigger no.

And ballroom dancing? Hell n—

Actually, Jamie thought, stopping short. Upon further reflection that one would probably be nice. Particularly if he'd be taking lessons with Audrey as his partner. His gaze slid over her small feminine frame, lingering broodingly on her de-lightful breasts and swept up over her plump bottom lip.

A dart of heat landed squarely in his groin and his palms suddenly itched with the unfamiliar need to cup her cheeks and draw her face up for his kiss. The Colonel had told him to do whatever it was he did to make a woman fall all over him, right? Well, kissing played a very significant part in that.

Unfortunately the Colonel had also forbidden First Base.

Audrey's suddenly heavy-lidded gaze dropped to his own mouth and, though it could have merely been wishful thinking on his part, she seemed to have leaned closer to him.

Then again, Jamie thought as his heart began to race and he lessened the distance between them a little more, the Colonel wasn't here. Jamie was on a mission and that mission was to prevent her from marrying the wrong guy. If he kissed her, that would help right?

Right.

Jamie stepped even closer, raised his hands and felt her hair slide across his knuckles. He hadn't even touched her, yet he could feel her warmth against his palms and the sensation made his stomach clutch. His hands found her face and—

"Woof!"

"Damn!" Jamie swore, startled by the deafening bark. He instinctively drew Audrey to him and frantically glanced around.

"Moses," she chided, turning to face her front door.

Jamie wilted—quite embarrassingly, considering he was supposed to be such a military bad-ass—and followed her gaze. The dog from the photo looked menacingly back at him. The enormous animal had both paws planted on the glass and stood an easy five and a half feet—taller than Audrey, he thought, wondering how the hell she controlled such a beast.

"He won't bite," she said. "He's just curious about you."

"Right," Jamie said warily, not trusting that assessment.

Cheeks pink, Audrey awkwardly peeled herself away from him and opened the door, allowing the dog outside. She patted his head. "*Friend,* Moses," she said sternly. "*Friend.*"

The dog ambled toward Jamie.

"Offer your hand."

Jamie shot her a hesitating glance. "Are you sure he won't mistake it for a chew toy?"

Audrey laughed. "Trust me, if he thought you were a threat, he would have torn your throat out by now."

Oh, now wasn't that a comforting thought? Jamie obligingly offered his hand. The dog sniffed his palm. Then his leg. Then his butt. Then predictably zeroed in on his crotch.

Chuckling again, Audrey grabbed Moses by the collar and tugged him back. "Good enough, old boy. Leave Jamie alone." She tucked her hair behind her ear. "Sorry about that," she mumbled, an adorable blush painting her cheeks.

Jamie couldn't think of anything politically correct to say, so he merely shrugged it off. "No problem. He's just being a dog."

She patted the dog again, then looked up, her wary gaze tangled with his. "Thanks for walking me home. It wasn't necessary."

Jamie shoved his hands in his pockets. "I enjoyed it. Well, most of it," he amended. "Your dog scaring the shit out of me, then molesting me I could have done without, but otherwise…" He grinned and shrugged.

A playful smile caught the corner of her lush mouth. "Too bad you aren't wearing one of those diapers, eh?"

Imp, Jamie thought, thoroughly enchanted and missing that might-have-been kiss. "Right."

"So I'll see you in the morning?"

"See you then," Jamie agreed. His heart curiously lighter than it'd been in months, Jamie loped down the steps and made his way toward his cottage. Adrenaline from the dog-scare still pumped through his veins, his dick throbbed painfully in his jeans and his body ached with the regret of leaving her.

But he was smiling. How screwed up was that?

6

AUDREY CLOSED THE DOOR behind her, dropped to her knees and gave Moses a grateful hug. A shaky breath leaked out of her lungs. "You saved me, big guy," she told him. "From doing something *really* stupid."

Moses licked her cheek in answer, causing an unexpected chuckle to break loose in her throat. "Oh, Moses," she said with a shaky laugh. "This isn't good."

And she was the master of understatement.

In fact, it was downright horrible.

Being attracted to Jamie Flanagan—and not just merely attracted, but devastatingly so—was so far wrong it should have been unthinkable—even though it wasn't.

In the first place, she was in a committed relationship, supposedly contemplating marriage to a man who expected an answer by the end of the week. And in the second place, this guy was a friend of her *grandfather's*.

And for whatever reason, that was the one that seemed like a bigger betrayal.

The Colonel had recommended and entrusted him into her care and she fully imagined that her seducing him, kissing him or having wild, wonderful sex with him was not the sort of relaxation therapy her grandfather'd had in mind. She knew all this and yet...

She couldn't seem to help herself from wanting it.

Audrey was a big girl. She was sexually experienced and sexually responsible. She didn't share her body with just anyone and she always made sure she was protected. She had too much self-respect to do otherwise. Though she longed to have a family of her own someday and imagined raising that family on this very shore, she instinctively knew that neither the time—nor sadly, the man—was right.

But nothing in her experience could have ever prepared her for the overwhelming do-or-die toe-curling attraction she felt for Jamie. He'd merely smiled at her and something about that lazy grin had tripped some sort of internal previously-undetected sexual trigger. Parts of her body which hadn't so much as tingled in years were suddenly vibrating with a twang of lust-ridden enthusiasm she could feel in her fillings…and other more erogenous places.

As for what almost happened on her porch, Audrey couldn't explain that either. One minute she'd been standing there, thinking about the rugged yet curiously vulnerable line of his cheek and the next, she'd found herself staring at his mouth.

Then gravitating toward that mouth.

But who could blame her? Honestly, the man had the most gorgeous lips she'd ever seen. They were surprisingly full for a guy, but masculine nonetheless. And when he smiled… Mercy, they were utterly devastating.

Those hungry eyes of his—an intriguing mixture of brown, gold and green—had boldly slid over her body, then sizzled a path over her breasts, up her neck and onto her lips. At that point, thinking for herself had become a thing of the past and she'd merely gotten caught up in the moment. The rest of the world had simply fallen away and nothing had existed but the two of them and the inevitable meeting of their mouths.

If Moses, God love his big drooling heart,

hadn't barked when he had, who knows what might have happened? They might have kissed, then kissed some more, and then she might have dragged him into the house, thrown him down onto the floor and ridden him until his eyes rolled back in his head. She might have had the most powerful orgasm of her life.

Forget the bed, forget a romantic fire, forget all the so-called set-the-mood trappings. She didn't—*wouldn't*—need them with him. She needed a hungry mouth, greedy talented hands and that impressive bulge she'd noticed when Moses had inspected his crotch. The mere memory made her laugh.

She pressed her forehead against his muzzle and lovingly scratched her dog behind the ears. "How was it?" she teased, stupidly envious of him.

All right, Audrey thought. Enough already.

Drawing in a cleansing breath, she reluctantly pushed herself to her feet, ambled over to her stereo and plugged in Anna Nalick, her newest artist obsession. She could listen to that melodious voice for hours on end and frequently did. Anna was young, but had a surprising maturity to her lyrics that rang truer than anything Audrey had heard in a long time.

"Breathe" came alive through the speakers and set the mood for her bath. By the time the final chord of the song sounded, Audrey was neck deep in apple-scented bubbles and she could feel the tension melting out of her body. At least most of it, at any rate. There was still a depressingly insistent throb in her sex, but it was nothing she couldn't take care of herself if it became downright unbearable.

Which was a distinct possibility, she thought, as her thighs tensed with the ache of unfulfilled expectation.

With a helpless half-laugh, half-sob, Audrey bit her bottom lip, then held her breath and sank beneath the water. She stayed there until her lungs burned and her focus had shifted to the ache in her chest, opposing the one in her loins. Ah, she thought, pushing the hair away from her face when she finally emerged from the water. Much better. Her lips formed a weak smile. Nothing like a little dunk to help one get their perspective in order. Drastic times called for drastic, not altogether sane, methods.

Did she still want Jamie? Of course. And she grimly suspected that the more time she spent with him, the more she could expect that malady to worsen. But at least her head was clear enough for the moment to try and put a defense in order, to get her head fully in the game, so to speak.

Because regardless of how badly she might want him, she'd never slept with a guest before and she damned sure wasn't going to start now.

Not this guy. Not this time.

Not Jamie Flanagan.

Yes, it was unfortunate that he'd mysteriously managed to awaken her inner porn star—when she hadn't known she'd even had one—but Audrey knew she'd simply have to wrestle her IPS back into submission with truckloads of guilt and a stringent professional attitude. Jamie was here because he needed help. Help, dammit, not sex.

Above all else, she needed to keep that in mind.

Furthermore, she needed to talk with her grandfather and find out exactly what had happened to Jamie's friend. Merely losing him couldn't account for that wretched sadness she'd glimpsed in those gorgeous eyes earlier this evening. Granted no doubt losing a close friend would have put it there, but not to the extent she'd seen—*or felt*. There was something more, something else that haunted him and dogged his every step. In fact, though the Colonel had sent him here, Audrey didn't think her grandfather was even aware of the full extent of Jamie's pain.

Clearly Jamie had gotten good at covering it up, but that's what most hurting guys did, right? If they couldn't beat the pain into submission, pound it into the ground or simply ignore it away, they hid it. God forbid they ask for help, she thought. Help indicated weakness. Jamie, in particular, she knew, wouldn't be able to stand that, perceived or otherwise. What the fool didn't realize was that it took strength to ask for help. Men, she thought with an eye roll. They had the emotional intelligence of a goat.

Audrey toed the drain open and levered herself out of the tub. She dried off, then wrapped herself in a towel and, rather than do the sensible thing like dress for bed, she strolled to her kitchen window, inexplicably drawn. After only a moment's hesitation, she nudged the curtain aside and stared down the hill toward Jamie's cottage.

To her surprise he was sitting on the topmost step of his porch. The light illuminated his impressive profile in stark relief, leaving the rest of him in dark shadow. A bottle of whiskey—the Jameson she'd had to special order for him—sat at his side, and he held a tumbler of the flickering amber liquid loosely in one hand, allowing it to dangle in the deep V between his thighs.

To a casual observer he appeared unguarded and relaxed, but for reasons which escaped her at the moment, she knew better. It was all part and parcel of the image he liked to portray. Or maybe *had* to portray to keep up the status quo? She sighed softly and rested her head against the glass. That seemed more likely.

If he held it together and pretended like nothing was wrong, then it wouldn't be. He'd be normal and the rest of the world could simply accept that he was fine, or they could go to hell. Audrey didn't have any idea where these impressions and feelings were coming from—she seemed to be more in tune with him than with anyone she'd ever met before—but she knew her instincts were right on. Felt the familiar weight of grief and emotion—*his grief and emotion*—seep into her very bones.

She was siphoning already, she realized with a flash of dread, and she'd barely spent any time with him. That certainly didn't bode well for the rest of the week.

God, why did this always happen to her?

Audrey thought with a silent whimper of despair. Why was she attracted to guys who used her up? Why couldn't she feel this overwhelming attraction for Derrick? Why didn't *he* make her heart squeeze with emotion and her thighs quiver with want?

Was she simply wired this way? she wondered. Could she only be attracted to men who needed her? How screwed up was that? How screwed up was *she?* It took very little insight to recognize that she was going to be taking a huge risk by working with Jamie. Between the off-the-Richter-scale attraction and this equally driving need to heal his hurts—even if that meant making them hers—she'd be a fool to think she wasn't teetering on a slippery slope.

And she was going to be damned lucky if she didn't fall.

Even worse…for him.

SINCE JAMIE HAD long ago learned to fall asleep in almost any position, in any condition, it was no surprise that he enjoyed a restful night. The mattress on his bed was just the perfect combination of soft and firm, the pillows were excellent and the sheets were quality—Egyptian cotton—

and had been cool and soft with a hint of some kind of summer rain scented fabric softener.

And the quarter bottle of whiskey he'd had before stumbling into bed hadn't hurt either.

He would have smiled, but knew from past experience that his face would hurt, so he quelled the urge. Instead, he braced both hands against the shower wall, bent his head and allowed the almost-scalding water to beat down on the back of his head and neck. Between the steam and two fingers of the hair of the dog, he was beginning to feel marginally better.

Jamie liked a drink as much as the next guy, but he ordinarily knew his limit. Hell, he'd been drinking Jameson since his grandmother had made him his first hot toddy. He knew when to stop. So why hadn't he, then? Jamie wondered, knowing the question was rhetorical.

He would have liked to blame it on the clear, cool night, the nocturnal sounds and lapping lake against the shore. Even better if he could have blamed it on boredom—he'd had nothing better to do than sit in the dark and get hammered.

But he knew better—he'd kept drinking because it had taken the edge off. The way Jamie had seen it, he'd had two choices. He could have either hiked back up the hill and finished what Moses had interrupted—and then some—or he could drink until he could master the urge.

While he hadn't mastered it by any stretch of the imagination, he'd at least managed to keep his feet planted firmly on the front porch of his "re-laxation" retreat. He smothered a snort. Hell, he'd been more relaxed behind enemy lines with rocket-powered grenades—RPG's in soldier speak—going off in his shadow.

Jamie turned the shower off, slicked his hair back from his face and snagged a towel from the rack. Now, in approximately sixteen minutes, if his internal clock could be trusted, he was supposed to continue this *relaxing* retreat painting watercol-ors—with Audrey, no less, so that she could person-ally witness his complete ineptitude—down by the lake.

Satan had a familiar and his name was Garrett, Jamie thought, with a bark of dry laughter which made his head threaten to split in two.

He'd fully expected a call from the devil last night, but he suspected a divine hand had inter-vened. Because if Garrett had dialed him up yes-terday evening, considering the alcohol pumping through his system, he would have most likely unloaded on him. Jamie had needed an outlet for all of this pent-up anxiety and since his preferred method of dealing with angst—sex, of course—was off-limits, that only left picking a fight. His cheeks puffed as he exhaled loudly. And since there was no one here he could reasonably pick a fight with—too bad Derrick had left, Jamie thought, wincing with regret—he'd had no choice but to drink.

The way he figured it, he was going to need a lot of alcohol to combat the attraction. If he factored in the time-to-attraction-to-alcohol ratio, then that meant he'd need an additional say…million bottles of whiskey to go with what he had left? If that didn't work, he could always see about being chemically castrated for the week. His lips quirked with miserable humor. A man had to have a plan, after all.

Feeling decidedly uninterested in watercolors, but ridiculously pleased to know that he'd see Audrey, Jamie dressed quickly and made his way outside.

"Ah," the object of his recent lust said. "There you are." Looking fresh and well rested and entirely too sexy for a woman dressed in an ugly flannel shirt, Audrey gestured to a wide assortment of gear at her hiking-boot clad feet. "Would you mind helping me with this stuff?"

"Sure," Jamie told her. He easily gathered a couple folding chairs and wooden easels into his arms, leaving her to tote a small bag he assumed held the rest of their painting necessities.

She shot him a curiously hesitant look. "Have you been up long?"

"A grand total of twenty-two minutes. Twenty of which were spent in the shower."

She smiled and inclined her head. "Ah," she sighed. "Slept well or barely slept?"

"Oh, I slept well."

"Good. Did you have time for breakfast?"

"Er…does thinking about it count?"

"No."

"Then no, I didn't have time for breakfast."

She shook her head. "Bad soldier," she chided. "My grandfather wouldn't approve. How does a muffin and some fruit sound?"

Not as good as a half a pound of bacon and a Spanish omelet, but better than nothing, he supposed, grateful nonetheless. "Good, thanks." What? Was she packing breakfast in that bag? he wondered.

Giving him a look he grimly suspected meant

she'd somehow read his mind, Audrey grinned and grabbed the radio attached to her waist. "Do you want anything to drink?"

"A beer would be nice."

"Not for breakfast. How does tomato juice sound?"

"Nasty. Can I have coffee?"

Eyes twinkling, she bit her lip. "Sure." She placed his order and asked that it be brought down to the lake. "There we go," she said. "Henry should be down in a few minutes."

"Thank you," he said, and meant it. It had been a long time since anyone had cared whether or not he'd eaten his Wheaties.

"No problem. Besides, it'll help metabolize that alcohol and get you over your hangover."

Startled, Jamie almost stumbled over his own feet. "I'm sorry."

She darted him a sly look over her shoulder. "No need to apologize."

"I wasn't apologizing. I just—" He chewed the inside of his cheek and, equally impressed and disturbed, considered her. "How did you know?"

She stopped at a level spot behind a rather thick copse of trees and dropped her bag, then took the chairs away from him. "Well, number one, you slept late and you're a military man—granted, one that's not currently in service—" she said before he could interrupt because he'd instantly readied his mouth for argument. "I know that's not the norm."

Good observation, he had to admit. Still, it wasn't enough to deduce a hangover.

She made quick work of setting up the chairs. "Secondly, you skipped breakfast and you appear entirely too health conscious to make that a regular habit."

On the money again, Jamie thought, feeling more and more transparent.

"Would you mind setting those up?"

He blinked. "Huh?"

She gestured toward the easels, forgotten in his hand. "Set those up, would you?"

Right, Jamie thought, jolting into action. His cheeks heated with embarrassment. Here she was doing all the work, while he stood rooted to the ground, marvelling over her ability to read him like a friggin' book. Good grief. He had to get his head out of his ass and into the game.

"And thirdly," she said, shooting him a mischievous smile. "You look like shit."

Since he was more accustomed to accepting compliments than criticism, the blunt insult took him completely by surprise, jarring a disbelieving chuckle loose from his throat. "Don't hold back," he told her dryly. "Tell me how you *really* feel."

She shrugged. "You asked me how I knew," she said. "Don't ask if you don't want to know."

Utterly intrigued by her, he pushed a hand through his hair and nodded. "Duly noted. Anything else I should know?"

"Nothing." She paused, then seemed to remember something important. "Oh, wait. Erm…I might have seen you on your front porch last night with that bottle of Jameson."

A slow smile spread across his lips. Ah, he thought. The heart of the matter. Now that made more sense. "You're a piece of work, you know that?"

She handed him a watercolor pad. "I might have heard that once or twice."

"Or more."

She nodded. "Or more."

Feeling like he'd moved back onto solid ground, Jamie flipped the pad open and arranged it onto the easel. He thought about pretending to know what to do next, but ultimately decided against it. What was the point? She knew perfectly well he didn't have any damned idea how to paint. "Okay. What now?"

Audrey bent down by the water's edge and filled two plastic cups. Now here was a perk, Jamie thought. She might be wearing the ugliest shirt in the Northern Hemisphere—one that was better suited to a lumberjack and not a woman who looked like a cover model—but that shirt was tucked into a pair of jeans which fitted her quite nicely. Her delectable ass presently tested the seams of the worn denim and he found himself silently wishing he had either X-ray vision or the ability to make her pants instantly vanish.

What the hell. Why not wish for both?

She'd tied her hair back into a long ponytail at the nape of her neck and the cool morning breeze flirted with the ends of her espresso curls. She looked sexy and competent and…wholesome, Jamie realized with a start.

Now there was a word he didn't usually associate with a woman he was attracted to. Stacked, sexy, dim—those were the qualities most of the women he hooked up with possessed. No muss, no fuss. Attraction, action, reaction, end of relationship.

Audrey, he knew, wasn't that kind of girl. And yet he wanted her more than he'd ever wanted another female in his life. Was it because he couldn't have her? The so-called thrill of the forbidden? Had Garrett's orders somehow made her even more attractive to him simply because he knew he wasn't supposed to touch her? His gaze slid over the delicate slope of her cheek, the curve of her brow, the dainty shell of her ear and his heart did a funny little squeeze he would have labeled indigestion had he eaten this morning.

That would have been the simple explanation—the one he wished like hell he could cling to—but he knew better. In an act of what he could only deduce as divine punishment for his mistreatment of women, the Almighty had placed him with the one woman in the world whom he instinctively knew could touch his soul…and had made her off-limits.

If that wasn't divine retribution he didn't know what was.

She straightened. "Now we paint," she said brightly.

Ah, yes. For a moment there he'd forgotten.

Audrey chuckled, the sound soft and curiously soothing to his ears. "Don't look so glum. Remember, this one is for my grandfather."

Jamie accepted his paints, brush and cup with a vengeful smile. "That's right," he told her. "He's got a fondness for orchids, right?"

"He does," she confirmed hesitantly. "But I thought you might want to paint the lake."

Jamie wet his brush and dipped it into the red, toyed around with the combination of pigment to water until he reached the right shade of pink. Pussy-pink, Jamie thought, stifling a chuckle. "Nope. I'll paint an orchid."

Clearly suspecting that he was up to something, Audrey slid him a guarded glance. "Suit yourself. I'm painting the lake."

"Good. It can be a gift for me."

A smile flirted with her lips while she played around with her paintbrush. "Why would I give it to you?"

He purposely let his gaze slide over her. "So I'll have a memento of you when I go home."

She cleared her throat. "And home's in Atlanta, right?"

"It is."

"My grandfather mentioned you'd left the military and had gone into a private security business with some friends. Also Rangers, right? In the same unit?"

He could only imagine what else he'd mentioned, Jamie thought. No doubt the sneaky bastard had told her about Danny, too. The thought had been offhand, but now that he truly considered it, Garrett would have most certainly told her about Danny. And if he'd told her about Jamie's friends, he'd *definitely* told her about Danny. Furthermore, he would have cited it as a reason for his visit. Jamie's fingers tensed around the brush and he mentally swore.

Repeatedly.

God, how could he not realize that before now? He suddenly felt exposed and vulnerable, two adjectives he'd just as soon not associate with himself. Danny's death was a private pain, one he had no intention of sharing with anybody. You know, it was one thing to send him up here to work some behind-the-scenes machinations to keep her from marrying an asshole, but to use his own grief as a means to that end was beyond the pale.

And Garrett had seriously underestimated him if he thought he would simply let that slide.

Belatedly remembering that he was supposed to be carrying on a conversation, Jamie finally managed to respond to her comment. "I *am* in the private security business," he confirmed. "With friends. Me and a couple of guys who were also under your grandfather's command opened up shop a few months ago."

"Congratulations."

"Thanks," he murmured, putting more effort into his painting. He wanted it to be *just* right for Garrett, the scheming bastard.

"And business is good?"

"Better than we expected," he told her, the pride evident in his voice.

"That's fantastic. It's nice when hard work pays off." She added a few strokes to her own work, then nibbled absently on the end of the brush. "Do you miss being a Ranger?"

That topic was still too raw and he didn't have a clear-cut answer he could give to himself, much less her. "Sometimes," he told her, for lack of anything better.

"I know what you mean." She cocked her head, studying her work. "In a previous life I was a commodities broker."

Now that was enough to draw him up short. Wearing what he knew had to be a dumbfounded look, Jamie paused and turned to stare at her. "You were a what?"

She chuckled at the look on his face. "A commodities broker. Had the whole Wall Street walk going on. The briefcase, the PDA, the BlackBerry."

"Seriously?"

"Seriously," she told him.

Jamie returned his attention to his orchid—which was beginning to finally resemble the female genitalia he'd been aiming for—and digested this newest bit of information about Audrey. He couldn't make it fit. "So how does a Wall Street commodities broker end up in Maine running a de-stressing camp?" he asked, genuinely intrigued. That was a big damned leap.

"If I told you that, I'd have to kill you," she teased. She sidled over next to him. "What are you—" She gasped, clasped her hand to her mouth to smother a laugh. "That looks like a—" Her shocked gaze swung to his.

Jamie quirked an eyebrow.

"I mean to say, that's… Well, that's—" She nodded, seemingly at a loss. "That's lovely."

Jamie grinned and chewed the inside of his cheek. "Is there something *wrong* with my orchid?"

She pressed her lips together, shook her head. "Not at all."

"I think he should hang it in a place of honor, don't you?" Jamie asked her sweetly. "Like behind his desk or maybe in his home office. Possibly even his bedroom."

Her cheeks pinkened adorably and she gazed at

his vagina painting with something akin to humorous outrage. "I'm s-sure he'll find a g-good home for it."

"You look a little flushed," Jamie commented, thoroughly enjoying her discomfort. "Are you feeling all right?" he asked with faux concern.

Tearing her fascinated blue gaze away from his painting, she jerked her attention back to him. "Me? Oh, no. I'm fine. Look," she said, a little too brightly. "There's Henry with breakfast."

If she'd been drowning, Henry would have been the lone life preserver in dangerous waters, Jamie thought, his lips curling into a grim.

"Oh, good," he enthused. "After I eat, I think I'll paint a picture of a couple of mountains. You know, the Colonel was right. This painting is. *very* relaxing."

7

"WHAT THE HELL do you think you're doing?" Tewanda said, under her breath. She gestured disgustedly at Audrey's clothes. "Flannel?" she asked, horrified. "*Flannel,* Audrey? Why on earth would you clothe yourself in the single greatest 'do-not-touch-me' fabric known to mankind when a hot man like that is here?"

That's exactly why she did it, Audrey thought, shooting a careful look at Jamie from the corner of her eye. He'd finished his *orchid* painting—she inwardly snorted—and was presently hard at work on his interpretation of "mountains." Despite the flannel shirt, she kept feeling his darting gaze study her breasts, then go back to work. It was enough to make a perfectly sane woman go a little crazy.

Though she'd been absolutely appalled at first, she had to admit the watercolors he was doing for her grandfather were excellent retribution for the various books and medications the Colonel had made sure were on hand for Jamie when he got here. She smiled and shook her head. Oh, but to be a fly on the wall when her grandfather opened those packages, she thought, stifling another chuckle.

"What the hell is wrong with you?" Tewanda snapped. "I'm not being funny. I'm serious. Stop smiling."

Audrey made an attempt to accommodate her overwrought friend. She flattened her lips and tried to pay attention.

She failed.

Tewanda shook her head. "I don't understand you," she said, seemingly summoning patience from a higher power. "You're either looking to replace the guy on *Home Improvement*, you've become a lesbian, or you're purposely dressing like this to make yourself unattractive." Her lips curled with knowing humor. "And my money's on the last one."

Then that was a good bet, Audrey thought. This morning when she'd gotten up, she'd actually agonized over what to wear. She'd tried on several outfits, made a mess of her closet and her room— which had taken a solid fifteen minutes to repair—

and generally acted like a junior high drama queen getting ready for her first date.

Which was ridiculous when she already had a boyfriend, dammit, and was not under any circumstances going to act on this unholy attraction to Jamie. If she could have clothed herself in burlap this morning, she would have done it.

That's how desperate she was.

And it wasn't that she didn't trust him. She didn't trust herself.

She'd stood at her kitchen window last night and gazed at him until that throb between her legs had beaten an insistent tattoo against her defenses and had, predictably, become unbearable. Audrey let go a small sigh. Thus, she'd ended up taking matters into her own hands.

Quite frankly, since Derrick wasn't an altogether guaranteed orgasm, self-service for her wasn't an uncommon occurrence. Furthermore, there was a distinct amount of satisfaction which came from knowing she wasn't dependent upon a man for her own release. Too bad that younger girls weren't encouraged to explore their bodies the way that young boys were expected to explore theirs, she thought.

Masturbation in guys was a forgone conclusion and yet for many girls, it was still considered taboo. Considering it took a great deal more finesse for a woman to achieve climax than a man, it would seem that girls should be encouraged to explore themselves with the same zeal in which boys did. But that was a whole other matter, Audrey thought, a double standard that she imagined was going to take decades to correct.

The point was, this was the first time Audrey had taken care of business with a specific man in mind and the result had been quite…spectacular. Beyond anything she could have expected. In addition, though it had dulled the edge, so to speak, the ache had immediately returned with a vengeance. If thinking about doing it with him could make her fly into a million pieces and melt against her mattress, then what would actually being with him do to her?

And if he didn't stop sending her those sexy half-smiles and sidelong glances, she wasn't merely going to have to wonder—she'd have to *know*.

And that, she knew, was out of the question.

Of course, it'd be easier to remember that if he'd quit flirting with her. She looked down at the ugly flannel shirt and winced. Clearly her plan wasn't working.

"Go change," Tewanda told her. "It's not too late. You're spending the whole day with him. Has he asked for that massage yet?"

"No," Audrey said, releasing a shaky breath at the mere thought of her hands sliding over that silky skin and muscle. "And I hope he doesn't." She whacked Tewanda against the arm.

"Ouch," Tewanda yelped accusingly, rubbing the spot. "What the hell was that for?"

"That was for suggesting I give him a massage. Carlos can give him a massage. Not me."

"Hunh." She shook her head. "That man is not going to let another man give him a massage."

"He will if he wants one bad enough," Audrey said. She needed to keep her hands to herself, thank you very much, and it was going to be hard enough without Tewanda's interference. Honestly, she'd known that her friend didn't care for Derrick, but she didn't realize just how much Tewanda hated him until Jamie had come along.

Derrick had called last night immediately following Audrey's help-yourself-orgasm buffet and she'd felt so guilty over fantasizing about Jamie that she hadn't answered the phone. Of course, the instant his accusatory "Where-are-you? Why-aren't-you-waiting-on-my-call?" tone had sounded through the small speaker, she'd immediately let go of any remorse.

"My mountains are done," Jamie called from over his shoulder.

Tewanda frowned. "Mountains?"

"Don't ask," Audrey said, laughing under her breath.

"Oh, now you can't laugh like that, then tell me not to ask." Tewanda squinted down the hill at Jamie, trying to make out his painting. "What's going on?"

Audrey nodded her head in Jamie's direction. "He's painted some special…*artwork* for my grandfather."

"How nice," Tewanda said, brightening. "The Colonel should like that."

"Mmm-hmm." Audrey crossed her arms over her chest. "Why don't you trot down there and take a look and then we'll see if you still think he'll like it."

With a haughty look of sheer bafflement, Tewanda did just that. Audrey quietly followed, looking forward to hearing her friend's take on Jamie's paintings.

"Do you mind if I take a look?" Tewanda asked him.

Jamie glanced past Tewanda and his twinkling

gaze tangled with hers. "Not at all," he said. "Art is meant to be shared, after all," he drawled.

Still smiling, Tewanda sidled forward and inspected the painting on the easel. The smile froze comically and she cocked her head and squinted, seemingly trying to make Jamie's mountains into, well…mountains. Her eyes widened and a shocked laugh burst from her throat when she realized what she was looking at. "Oh, you did not!" she said, her voice equally flabbergasted and impressed.

Jamie chuckled at her. "Want to see my orchid?" he offered.

One look at the orchid made Tewanda dissolve into a fit of hysterical laughter. "He'll have your beautiful white ass drawn and quartered for this, you know," she finally told him when she could speak.

Jamie inclined his head. "Probably."

"You don't look nearly as worried as you should," she added.

"Nothing worries me much anymore," Jamie said lightly, but there was a truth in the humor which somehow rang very honest. It was a telling statement, Audrey thought, and filed it away for future consideration.

Tewanda sighed regretfully. "I've got to get

back to work," she said with one last look at Jamie's orchid.

"Radio me if you need me," Audrey told her.

She laughed. "Don't I always?"

Audrey sidled into her friend's vacated spot next to Jamie and inspected the mountains for herself. Like the orchid, there was a surprising amount of detail which told her that, while he definitely was a novice painter, he had quite a knack for capturing the female form. And since he was painting from memory, well… She instinctively knew he'd never leave a girl hanging.

He would be a guaranteed orgasm.

The mere knowledge made a shiver work its way through her.

"You cold?" Jamie asked.

Audrey shook her head, trying to clear it of before and after orgasmic visions of her and Jamie. "No, I'm fine." She drew a bracing breath. "So…are you finished painting or would you like to try your hand at a banana?"

His eyes crinkled at the corners. "I'll save the banana for later in the week."

A self-portrait? Audrey wondered, her mouth watering. "All right, then. Let me take a look at your schedule and see what you're supposed to do next."

Jamie rinsed his brush off, then disposed of the water in the cup. "Aren't you going to ask me what I want to do next?" he asked. He'd lowered his voice an octave and a curious invitation, one that made the hairs on the back of her neck stand on end, rang through the deep, sexy baritone.

She paused, toying with the necklace around her throat. "I'm hoping you're going to want to follow along with the schedule, but if it makes you feel better to tell me what you want to do, then by all means, go ahead."

"Where's Moses?" he asked, moving closer to her.

Audrey felt her brow wrinkle. "He's at home."

"Locked up tight, then?"

"Er…yeah."

She lost a little more of her personal space as he crowded even closer in. "Can't escape and tear my throat out?"

"No," she said hesitantly.

Jamie's finger slid up her neck, tilting her face closer to his, and rested under her chin. "Can't interrupt?"

"R-right," she murmured shakily, utterly mesmerized and rooted to the spot.

"Then, if you have no objections, I'd like to

pick up where we left off last night," he murmured softly, weaving his voice and the image he'd effortlessly conjured around her senses. His warm breath fanned against her lips and his body heat seemed to be magically absorbed into her own hot spots. Her nipples tingled, her belly grew muddled, and that throb in her womb hammered until she wasn't altogether sure remaining upright without his support was going to be possible.

"Can I kiss you, Audrey?" he whispered, asking permission, of all things, when he could surely tell she had no objections. Making the choice completely hers. It was old-fashioned and noble and her heart squeezed with the kindness behind the gesture.

"Y-yes," she breathed, unable to conjure the sane response.

And God help her, that was the last fully-formed thought before his lips touched hers and life as she'd known it abruptly ended.

JAMES AIDAN FLANAGAN had stolen his first kiss in third grade from a blue-eyed blonde who'd smiled with angelic wonder after his bold preemptive move—then immediately thereafter cold-cocked him for his impertinence. His nose had bled for half an hour and his mother—probably the hardest working person he'd ever known—had had to leave her job and come to the school for a "meeting" on his behalf.

Jamie had learned two important lessons from that singularly defining experience.

One, never take anything without asking first.

And two, there was no action without consequence and sometimes those consequences weren't your own.

As a result of his stunt, his mother had had to pay for that thirty minutes of lost time with an extra shift, or lose her job. Though his grandmother had insisted that he go to bed that night, Jamie hadn't slept, and when his mother's tired footsteps had brought her into his room later that evening and he'd felt her fingers brush his cheek and glimpsed her weary loving smile, his chest had ached with the weight of guilt.

Curiously, though tasting Audrey—savoring her sweet breath and the plum-soft texture of her lips—was one of the most phenomenal gut-wrenchingly perfect experiences of his life, that same weighty ball of guilt he'd noted at eight had taken up residence in his belly. The meaning was clear—he might not have taken her kiss without permission, but he had a grim suspicion that she'd be paying for the consequences of his actions.

A better man would stop now, wouldn't be dragging her closer to him, angling her head to more fully devour her. A better man would stop, or more importantly, would have never have started. And let's face it, a better man wouldn't have agreed to the Colonel's scheme at all, admiring the purpose but refusing to participate.

But if being a better man meant he'd never feel these small hands pushing into his hair, tasting the gentle pleasure of her breath, the silken slide of her tongue into his mouth, then Jamie would simply have to resign himself to being a self-serving bastard. Because he couldn't stop now if his life depended on it.

Unlike a lot of men who merely used kissing as a means to an end, Jamie had always enjoyed it. While he wouldn't go so far as to say that kissing was as good as sex, he would say that it was second in line to the most personal...and telling. A guy could learn a lot about what sort of lover a woman would be by her kiss. In fact, a sorry kisser almost always resulted in a sorry lover.

It was no surprise then, given how potent his

initial attraction and curiosity about Audrey had been, that the meeting of their mouths could be anything short of extraordinary.

And it was also no surprise that she was the single most talented kisser he'd ever had the pleasure of tangling tongues with. Kissing her was a full-body experience. He felt the effects of her lips in every cell in his being. His hands shook, his dick throbbed, his belly inflated with what felt like fizzy air and the rest of him seemed to be melting. Her technique was flawless. She was ardent and energetic, sensual and sure.

But most importantly, she didn't try to pretend like she wasn't equally affected.

He could feel her beaded nipples through the flannel, raking against his chest. Flannel suddenly became his favorite fabric, Jamie decided as he slid a hand down her tiny back, then over her sweetly curved rump. She slithered and squirmed, positioning herself as closely to him as she possibly could. Her hands alternately kneaded his scalp and shaped his jaw, forcing him to accept her ministrations. Every mewl and sigh of pleasure echoed off his tongue and it took every iota of willpower he possessed to not topple her to the ground and bury himself inside her.

Just like their kiss, he knew it would be instinctively explosive.

Jamie wouldn't have thought a bolt of lightning could have startled them apart, but ironically, a single ring of his cell phone did.

Audrey stilled in his arms, then quietly stepped back. In a second, he watched the passion fade from her gaze and a cloud of worry and regret take its place.

He inwardly swore, checked the display, then swore aloud when he recognized the caller.

Garrett.

The man clearly had some sort of psychic connection, Jamie thought, resisting the ridiculous urge to scan the tree line. "Flanagan," he finally answered, his voice a bit rusty to his own ears.

"Where's my granddaughter?"

Jamie's gaze slid to Audrey. "Standing right here," he replied. "Would you like to talk to her?"

"Now that was subtle, Flanagan," he said, annoyed.

"Sorry, sir," Jamie lied dutifully. "What can I do for you?"

An exasperated sigh hissed over the line. "I just wanted to check in and see how things were going. Are you making any progress yet?"

Oh, yeah, Jamie thought, his gaze sliding over Audrey's slightly swollen lips. He could say that. "Yes, sir. I'm enjoying myself," he said, opting to play along and keep up the ruse. In for a penny, in for a pound, he supposed.

Especially now.

"Excellent. Has she confided anything about Derrick yet? Told you that he's proposed?"

"No, sir. The weather's beautiful. We've been painting and I've—" Jamie smothered a chuckle. "I've made a couple of things for you." He aimed a smile at her and was relieved when a ghost of a grin caught her lips as well. "Audrey has kindly offered to have them framed and shipped to you."

"Well, just keep plugging along," Garrett told him. "You haven't been there a full twenty-four hours yet. Even with your legendary charm, I didn't expect her to fall at your feet."

How odd, Jamie thought, when just a second ago she'd been standing on them to get closer to his mouth. Somehow he didn't think Garrett would appreciate that little nugget of information, though, so he decided to keep it to himself.

"Right, sir."

"You've got to make this work, Flanagan," Garrett told him grimly. "Failure is not an option here. According to my sources, Derrick is so sure of Audrey's answer that he's already bought a ring and booked a venue." He growled low in throat. "The arrogant SOB."

Jamie silently concurred. He glanced at Audrey and tried to imagine her married to Derrick and discovered, quite disturbingly, that he couldn't imagine her married to anyone…but himself. Which was ridiculous when he had absolutely no intention of ever marrying anyone.

Period.

Furthermore, he'd just met her. Soul-soothing eyes and flaming attraction aside, thinking about any form of permanent attachment was *extremely* premature. He was losing his mind, Jamie decided. She'd gotten him so damned hot she'd evidently rewired his brain.

Garrett cleared his throat. "Do your job, Flanagan," he told him. "And don't forget my orders. On deck but never up to bat. You haven't forgotten, have you?"

Jamie's conscience twinged. He passed a hand over his face. "No, sir."

"Good," the Colonel groused. "I'm fond of you, Flanagan. I'd hate to have to kill you." With that, he disconnected.

Evidently unable to stand still, Audrey had gathered their watercolor gear while he'd been on the phone. She folded the final chair and added it to the stack. "Checking in on you, eh?" she asked, obviously going to pretend that their scorching kiss had never happened.

Up on him was more like, but Jamie merely nodded. "Yeah."

Audrey hefted the bag onto her shoulder and frowned. "He's been acting weird lately," she said. A droll smile tugged at her lips. "He and Tewanda have spent entirely too much time on the phone for my comfort recently."

Jamie grabbed the remaining painting para-phernalia and fell in behind her as she made her way back up the hill. "Oh?"

"Yeah." She started to say something, but quickly changed her mind. She gave her head a small shake. "It's nothing, I'm sure." She shot him a smile. "I'm just being paranoid."

No, she wasn't, Jamie thought, feeling even more like a snake in the grass. She was reading everything correctly, but the signals just weren't clear enough for her to realize what was going on. God help Garrett—and himself—if she ever *did* realize what they'd been up to. While Audrey might come across as easygoing and mild mannered, he had the distinct impression that she could very quickly unload…and hold a grudge.

She'd forgive the Colonel—he was her grandfather, after all, and had her best interests at heart—but she would never forgive him, Jamie realized.

She'd hate him.

And the kicker was…he'd deserve it.

8

*****

"DON'T BE GENTLE, CARLOS," Audrey said, sighing with pleasure as Unwind's resident masseur used his magic hands on her shoulders. The soothing sound of bubbling water and the pungent aroma of relaxing herb-scented candles wrapped around her senses. If she didn't have so much on her mind—namely a six and half foot Irish American with miracle lips and the best ass she'd ever seen—she'd undoubtedly take a little catnap. As it was…

"Okay, then," he said, upping the pressure. "You asked for it. Geez, I haven't seen you this tense since that week we had the Slim-It-Up Diet group here."

"God, don't remind me," she groaned, her face pressed into the hole of the massage table. "Those women were horrible." And that was an understatement. They'd driven Tewanda stark raving mad with their low-fat no-fat strictly-organic *screw-it-where-the-hell-are-the-candy-bars?* demands.

Carlos clucked his tongue. "Hungry women are bitches."

She grunted. "Hungry women are insane. They broke into the kitchen. Remember that?"

He chuckled, working on a particularly tense spot between her shoulder blades. "I'd forgotten about that," he mused aloud. "That diet was too stringent. No wonder they snapped." He sighed. "Everything in moderation, I always say."

Yeah, well, that only worked if you only liked things in moderation, Audrey thought, guiltily picturing the half-pound block of chocolate in her bedside drawer. No one ever wanted good stuff in moderation, and those who did were…boring, she decided. To her dismay, an image of Derrick leaped instantly to mind, bringing guilt right along with it. She determinedly pushed both away, unwilling to devote any brain-power to what she knew would be a sobering thought process.

Say what you wanted about those dieters, but at least they were *passionate*. They knew what they wanted and had the guts to go after it. What if Monet hadn't painted in excess? If Beethoven had only been moderately motivated to compose? What if she did exactly what she wanted and seduced the hell out of Jamie Flanagan without the slightest notion of right, wrong and consequences?

What if she threw every bit of good sense and caution to the wind and didn't consider the repercussions of her actions at all? As if there wasn't a Derrick? As if Jamie wasn't her grandfather's friend? What if she did exactly what those passionate dieters had done and just said to hell with all of it? She let go a whimper. Would that be so terribly wrong?

Carlos paused. "You say something?"

She blushed. "No."

She was in hell, Audrey decided. And considering parts of her were still feverish and she'd left Jamie more than an hour ago, she imagined things were only going to get worse. Honestly, finishing out the day with him after that meltdown of a kiss—hell, she'd practically scaled his body, trying to get closer to him—had been sheer torture. Rather than dealing with the situation like an adult, she'd pretended like it had never happened. Pathetic? Juvenile? Cowardly? Yes…but she couldn't help it.

That timely call from her grandfather had been like a well-planned, well-aimed hose. Nothing could snuff out a blaze of lust faster than a hefty dose of guilt, that was for damned sure. As a result of her grandfather's call, Audrey had forced herself to focus on helping Jamie, the real reason he was here, after all.

Granted it had been difficult—she couldn't look at his face without zeroing in on that mouth, particularly after what had happened down by the lake—but fortunately, the Lord had blessed her with a very stubborn nature. When she truly set her mind to something, she could typically make it work.

Besides, she was genuinely curious and, after glimpsing his pain, genuinely concerned. No doubt Jamie's special forces training had included how to handle an interrogation because every single time she'd attempted to bring the conversation back around to his military career, he'd shut down and charmingly changed the subject. At one point, he'd given her a probing gaze which led her to believe that he knew exactly what she was fishing for, but wasn't going to be baited into giving it to her. While he hadn't overtly smirked at her, that's exactly what it had felt like.

Ordinarily she'd opt for the patient approach, but for whatever reason, she knew that wasn't going to work with him. Audrey frowned, considering. He was too controlled, too far into denial. In too much pain. No, patience definitely wasn't going to be the key in his case. It would take persistence. She'd simply have to keep asking questions, keep hammering away, adding to the pressure and he'd tell her to go to hell.

Or he'd explode.

And who knew? Audrey thought with a silent chuckle. He might do both. But she wasn't going to stop until she got something from him. Whatever his problem, it was festering inside him and, whether he knew it or not—or wanted to or not—he needed to let it go. Did she expect him to forget his friend? No, of course not.

But Jamie's hurt went far deeper than typical grief and holding onto that pain was much more destructive than allowing himself to heal. He was punishing himself, purposely, she suspected. Atonement for some sort of sin? Audrey wondered. Guilt? And if so, for what?

"Relax," Carlos chided.

Audrey frowned, unaware that she'd tensed back up. She took a deep breath, allowing her muscles to loosen once more. "Sorry," she mumbled.

Carlos's soft chuckle sounded in the relative silence. "No worries," he teased. "How can you expect the guests to adhere to our motto when the owner doesn't?"

A long futile sigh leaked out of her lungs. "The owner never does, otherwise people here wouldn't have 'no worries.'"

He tsked. "Now that doesn't sound fair."

Audrey felt her lids flutter shut and a small smile curled her lips. "Haven't you heard? Life's not fair."

Carlos slid his thumbs down her spine, his signature "massage over" ending. "There you go, sweetheart. I hope you feel better."

Audrey gingerly levered herself into a sitting position. "I do, thanks," she said, pushing her hair away from her face. She wrapped the sheet tighter around her body and slid off the table. The tile was cool beneath her bare feet.

"Man or money?"

She blinked. "I'm sorry?"

Carlos sent her a thoughtful glance. "When a woman is as tense as you are, it's either a man or it's money." He smiled and shrugged. "Since business is good, I'm going to go out on a limb here and say that it's a man." He paused. "And since I know you need me, I'm going to saw it off and say it's not Derrick."

Audrey considered feigning outrage, but couldn't summon the energy. What was the point? Carlos was right. She *did* need him. He was a thirty-four-year-old Cuban American who was handsome enough to make her female clientele happy, but manly enough to put most of the men who came through camp at ease—and made some of the men who came through camp swoon. Frankly, Audrey had no idea whose team he batted for and she didn't care. He was charming, dependable and competent. Furthermore, he was a friend.

"What makes you so sure that it's not Derrick?" Audrey asked, intrigued.

"In my line of work, there's tension…and then there's *tension*," he told her, his lips twisting with knowing humor. "You've been seeing Derrick for more than a year, but in all that time you've never been wound so tight that a quick trip over a set of railroad tracks would set you off. Derrick doesn't have that—" his lips twitched "—*effect* on you."

"Carlos!" Audrey admonished, feeling her face flame. Good grief. Was she that transparent? Did she have "I need an orgasm from Jamie Flanagan" plastered on her forehead?

"Save that tone for Tewanda," he said, tossing a towel over his shoulder. "Denial's bad for your complexion. Are you drinking enough water? You look a little flushed."

"Shut up," Audrey replied, exasperated.

"Get laid," Carlos shot back, chuckling. "You know you want to."

"What I want to do and what I should do are two completely different things."

"Cop-out."

"It's not a cop-out," she said shrilly. "It's—" She gestured wildly, searching for the correct response. "It's being an adult."

He shrugged, unconcerned. "It's being a coward."

Sending Carlos an annoyed look, Audrey took a deep breath, counted to five, then let it go. She definitely needed to check on that death penalty thing because throttling her help was becoming an almost overwhelming temptation.

"I'm not afraid," she said, chewing the words lest her temper get the better of her. "I'm cautious. There's a difference."

"Cautious, eh?" he asked, seriously now, his

gaze soft and somehow pitying. "And where's that gotten you?"

Audrey swallowed, recognizing the truth that lay unspoken between them. They both knew where being cautious had gotten her—with an arrogant egomaniac who didn't ignite any of her passions and who planned to dump her at the end of the week if she refused to marry him. That's what being cautious had done for her. Audrey chuckled darkly, released a low sigh and dropped her head.

Carlos walked over, tilted her chin up and planted a sweet, friendly kiss on her forehead. The gesture made her eyes inexplicably water and a lump swell in her throat.

"Sorry to hold up a mirror, babe, but someone's gotta do it," he said. "You want him, take him," he urged. "What's the worst that can happen?"

Audrey laughed, shook her head at the futility of it all. "You hit the nail on the head, Carlos," she said with a melancholy smile. "*That's* what I'm afraid of."

FROM THE CORNER OF HIS EYE Jamie watched Audrey try to covertly study the basket he was presently—much to his displeasure—weaving.

He was quite obviously not following the pattern which had come with his kit and, being as she was a very observant person, she'd no doubt noticed his…modifications. He waited, instinctively knowing that she wouldn't be able to resist "helping" him. His lips twitched with a smile.

After all, that's what she did, what she was best at. Thus far he'd managed to thwart every casually veiled attempt to draw him out, but as he was her new project, so to speak—and he was so obviously screwed up—he knew that she'd officially taken him under her wing and had become one of those damaged men she was self-destructively drawn to.

Needless to say, it galled him to no end.

And despite Garrett's assertion that he'd chosen Jamie for this mission because of his player reputation, Jamie fully believed now that Garrett had chosen him for another reason. He hadn't sent Jamie in solely because he'd thought Jamie could charm her—he'd sent him because he knew she wouldn't be able to resist *fixing him*. Amazing what sort of clarity could come from being half-loaded, Jamie thought.

Last night had been another drink-himself-into-numbness act of futility. Hell, even the best Irish whiskey couldn't dull this ache. If he'd been thinking clearly before he kissed her, he would have realized that, but considering that anything remotely resembling coherent judgment had eluded him since he'd met Audrey, that was equally pointless.

At any rate, he knew she wasn't going to stop trying to make him share his past—or God forbid, his feelings, Jamie thought, stifling a wave of panic—so he'd decided that she'd left him with no choice but to up his offensive.

In short, despite Garrett's warning, he was going to stage a full-out no-holds-barred seduction.

Let Garrett castrate him, Jamie thought, because it was definitely better than the alternative. He didn't want to be *fixed,* thank you very much. He was fine. He'd lost a friend. He was grieving, dammit. Why couldn't everyone just accept it and let him deal with things in his own time? If he tagged every woman from here to Borneo, it was nobody's damned business. His gaze slid to Audrey and he broodingly considered her.

Furthermore, he'd castrate his own damned self before he became her *pity* project.

The way Jamie figured it, she needed to focus her energy elsewhere. If she wasn't willing to do it on her own, then he'd simply have to help her. She wanted him. He knew it. He could feel it every time that clear blue gaze slid over him. His skin practically sizzled in its wake. He'd tasted it in her kiss, felt her breasts pearl against his chest. In fact, the only thing that made being here bearable was knowing that she wanted him as much as he wanted her.

Audrey hesitated, then predictably scooted closer to him and inspected his work. "Did you abandon your pattern on purpose?" she asked.

Jamie chewed the inside of his cheek. "I did."

"Oh," she said. "You're doing quite well. I thought you'd said you'd never done this before."

Jamie didn't look up, but continued to work. Hell, if he could assemble a weapon in under sixty seconds, he could weave a damned basket without following a pattern. Besides, this, too, was another gift to Garrett and he somehow didn't think that they made a pattern for one shaped like a pair of testicles. "I haven't."

She hesitated again, bit her lip. "Then don't you think you'd be better off following the instructions the first time?" she asked gently.

"I don't follow instructions well."

"You were a Ranger. You're not like the typical man. You have to follow instructions."

"I followed *orders*," Jamie clarified. "Not instructions."

A smile rolled around her lips. "And there's a difference?"

Jamie pulled in a deep breath, let it go with a whoosh and then smiled at her. "It's subtle."

"Oh," Audrey said, laughing. "Thanks for clearing that up for me. I had no idea."

"Most women don't."

"Ouch," she teased, feigning offense.

"Present company excluded, of course," Jamie told her. He continued to work the reed through his frame, and nodded in approval when his new present for the Colonel began to take proper shape.

"Does it come naturally to you, I wonder, or did you have to take a special class?" she asked conversationally, working on her own design. They presently sat at a table on her front porch. She'd ordered a nice breakfast this morning, which they'd shared, and Moses—who'd immediately gone for his crotch again the instant he'd arrived—currently lay sprawled across her feet. If he wasn't so sexually frustrated and constantly on guard, he would have said that this was…nice.

Jamie frowned. "Did I take what class?"

"Bullshit 101. Honestly, I don't think I've ever heard anyone quite as good at BS as you are."

A startled laugh bubbled up his throat. "Oh, I didn't have to take a class. I'm a natural when it comes to bullshit."

Blue eyes twinkling, she shot him a grin. "Well, I suppose everyone has to have a special talent."

Jamie help couldn't himself, that opening was just too perfect to resist. "BS is an art." He chuckled wickedly and lowered his voice. "You haven't seen *my* special talent…but I'd certainly be willing to show you."

In fact, he had every intention of showing her over and over again. Quite frankly, he'd like nothing better than to show her right now, but he suspected if he so much as made a move near her, dear old Moses would obligingly tear his throat out.

Predictably, she flushed. She blinked as though suddenly disoriented and he had the privilege of watching her pulse suddenly flutter wildly at the base of her throat. God, how he wished he could taste it. Taste her all over. His dick leaped in his jeans and a hot, achy throb pulsed in his loins, forcing him to grit his teeth. He wanted her so much that even his chest ached, in the vicinity of his heart if he could admit he had one. Did that scare the hell out of him? Most certainly. His heart had absolutely no business in this.

But if he'd ever wanted another woman more— had ever been so obsessed with marking her as his—Jamie couldn't recall it. This force that was pulling him toward her…it was more than mere attraction. Attraction he could deal with—*need,* on the other had, posed a problem and that's what this felt like.

He didn't just want her—he had to have her. He wanted to take her hard and fast, then slow and easy. He wanted to settle her over his thighs, impale her on his dick, then suckle her breasts until she screamed his name. He wanted to wring her dry, then whet her appetite again. He wanted to take her so hard that the idea of ever being with anyone else would be jarred right out of her beautiful head.

And for reasons which were absolutely beyond his understanding, he wanted to punish her for making him want her so much. When this was over, he may finally have to break down and see a shrink, Jamie decided. In the meantime, he was going back to what had worked before—sex therapy.

Audrey finally cleared her throat. "So," she said, in an unnatural high-pitched voice. "If you aren't making the Country Onion basket, then what sort are you making?" She frowned. "It looks like you've got an egg there that didn't split."

"Close," Jamie said. "It's a testicle basket."

Audrey's eyes widened in shock and she choked. "A what?"

Jamie grinned. "It's another gift for your grand-father. I was thinking about crocheting some little sperm to go in there for him, but since he didn't list needlework as one of my hobbies, I guess I'll have to settle for some sort of substitute. Any ideas?"

Still laughing, she sighed and shook her head. "Your last wishes, because if you send him this in addition to your orchid and mountains paintings, he's going to kill you." She paused. "Is it so bad being here?" she asked. The note of genuine interest and insecurity he detected in her voice prevented the glib comment he would have other-wise provided.

"No," Jamie said. He reached over and traced the pad of his thumb over her bottom lip. "Not when I'm with you." Now it was his turn to ask a question. "Do you regret kissing me yesterday?"

For whatever reason, her answer was far more important to him than he'd ever care to admit.

A shadow passed over her eyes and she hesitated. "Regret isn't the right word."

"I just wondered, you know, 'cause you keep trying to pretend like it never happened."

"It shouldn't have happened."

"So you do regret it."

"No," she said, giving her head a small helpless shake. "I enjoyed it too much to regret it. But I *should* regret it. I'm—" She winced, seeming to weigh her words carefully. "I have a boyfriend," she finally blurted out. "He's asked me to marry him and instead of thinking about my answer, I'm here kissing you. Guilt," she told him, apparently seizing the right word. "Guilt but not regret."

Ah, guilt. Jamie knew a lot about that. Still... "And there's a difference?" Jamie teased, throwing her earlier question back at her.

She smiled, just a simple matter of rearranging the muscles on her face, and yet he felt that grin tug at his midsection. "It's subtle," she told him, eyes twinkling with humor.

He inclined his head. "Looks like I'm not the only one who's a bit of a bullshit artist."

She shrugged, unrepentant. "I try," she demurred.

Unable to help himself, Jamie leaned forward and pressed a gentle kiss against her lips. Her sweet breath stole his. "Do you have plans for tonight?"

She blinked drunkenly, then a slow smile caught the corner of her mouth. "No."

"Excellent," Jamie told her. "I'll share my whiskey…and you can give me that massage."

9

"No, Gramps, he still hasn't told me anything," Audrey said, scattering olives over her salad. Dinner hadn't been part of the deal, but she'd been struck by the urge to cook. A blatant stall tactic, but what the hell? She was equally anxious and desperate.

"Nothing?" Evidently disheartened, the Colonel sighed. "I was hoping that he'd start to loosen up a little."

Oh, he had, Audrey thought, remembering that toe-curling kiss he'd given her this afternoon. Just not in the way that her grandfather had hoped for.

"It's going to take a little time, but I'm glad you called. I wanted to ask you something." She quickly washed her hands, then made her way into the living room.

"Sure. What's on your mind?"

Audrey hesitated. Now that she had the opportunity to find out a little more about Jamie's past, something about it felt wrong and intrusive. While she knew she'd be better able to help him if she had all of the information—and admittedly, she was curious—she nevertheless couldn't shake the feeling that she was mining for information he'd just as soon not share.

But the more time she spent with him, the more she saw how desperately he hurt. Had he told her anything? No. Trying to get that man to give her one single nugget of personal information beyond the superficial had been like trying to coax water from a stone—it wasn't happening.

He smiled, he laughed, he teased, he flirted.

And she lapped up every second of it, charmed in spite of her better judgment.

But he didn't give her anything he wasn't willing to share.

And while that might have worked with the average woman who was mesmerized by those gorgeous hazel eyes and bowled over by that extraordinary body and sex appeal, it wasn't working with her because she could *feel* his pain. And every second she spent in his company, every unguarded glimmer she caught—rare though they may be—only made the ache to soothe him worse. He might not know it, but he needed her.

"Sweetheart?"

Audrey blinked. "Yeah, I'm here. Listen, I need to know more. I know you told me that Jamie lost a friend, but I'm sensing there's more to it than that."

"What makes you say that?"

"I can feel it, Gramps," Audrey told him quietly. She didn't have to explain. He knew exactly what she was talking about. "A cold stone sits in my gut every time he slips up and lets me in." She plopped heavily onto her couch and patted the spot beside her for Moses. The great animal jumped up next to her and laid his enormous head on her thigh.

Her grandfather sighed heavily. "I was afraid of this. Is he too much, honey?"

"No," she assured him. "It's not that. It's—" How to explain? "I keep pressing and pressing, but I'm not getting anywhere. I need to know more."

"All right," he relented, clearly reluctant. "But this is strictly between us. If it comes down to it, I don't mind you telling him that I've told you that he lost a friend, but he would seriously object to my sharing the details."

"That's fine," Audrey said, bracing herself. Every muscle tensed in anticipation and she had to force her fingers to relax around the phone.

"Flanagan's unit was special," he began. "Elite. Secretive." He went on to tell her about how the four of them had met in ROTC in college, how they'd been more like brothers than friends, how their last mission had gone so terribly wrong, resulting in Daniel Levinson's death.

Her grandfather let out a tired breath, one that spoke eloquently to his age and burdens. "What I didn't tell you, Audie, is that it was Flanagan who went back to get Levinson when he went down. Amid enemy fire, no less. Unfortunately, Levinson had taken a fatal hit and he bled out in Flanagan's arms before Flanagan could get him off that hill."

"Oh, God," Audrey whispered, her chest squeezing painfully. Nausea threatened, forcing her to swallow.

"The other two—Payne and McCann—they took it hard as well, but Flanagan… Well, understandably, Flanagan hasn't been right since it happened. He and Levinson were supposed to have each other's back. He feels like he failed him. All of them do. That's why they wanted out."

She could certainly understand that. And knowing what she knew now, she could definitely see why Jamie was hurting so terribly badly.

Losing a friend would be hard enough, but feeling responsible, then having that friend die in your arms... She couldn't imagine. But she didn't have to because she could feel it emanating off of him.

"Thanks for telling me, Gramps. I, uh..." She scrubbed a hand over her face. "That, uh... That explains a lot."

"Keep me updated, would you?" the Colonel asked.

"I will," Audrey promised. She said goodbye, disconnected and then absently rubbed Moses' head, and continued to consider everything she'd just learned. Poor Jamie, Audrey thought, wincing for him. No wonder he was so closed-mouthed about all of it. Not only was it very private, but also, talking about it no doubt conjured images he'd just as soon forget. The trouble with that, though, was that he'd never forget. He might learn to deal with it—to cope, even—but the memories would always be there.

In fact, according to a recent study, memories in times of trauma were essentially *hard-wired* into the brain due to the additional adrenaline pumping through a person's body. Modern medicine was currently researching a pill which would ultimately help make traumatic memories fade. According to several well-known doctors, veterans, victims of horrific crimes such as rape and murder, would particularly benefit from it. Audrey let go a breath.

Unfortunately, there was no such magic pill yet for Jamie and he was simply going to have to learn to cope the old-fashioned way. She still felt guilty about asking her grandfather for that information, but she was glad that she did. It was easier to find something if you knew what you were looking for.

And she could start looking immediately, because Jamie would be here any minute now with his whiskey in tow. Despite everything she'd just found out, Audrey felt a half-hearted grin tease her lips. A miserable anxious laugh bubbled up her throat. Sweet Lord, what had she gotten herself into?

I'll share my whiskey...and you can give me a massage.

No doubt getting a buzz would help take the edge off the thought of putting her hands on him— just thinking about it made a quaking shiver rattle her belly—but she just hoped it didn't take the edge off too much. Oh, who the hell was she kidding? If he so much as crooked his little finger, she'd leap on him like a wild woman and he'd have a hell of a time getting her off.

They'd followed their basket-weaving lesson this morning with an amiable horseback ride around the lake, then had shared a late lunch in the lodge. Afterwards, Jamie had wanted to check out the gym and they'd spent the rest of the afternoon working out. Or rather, she had pretended to work out, and had watched him instead.

Mercy.

Watching Jamie Flanagan work out was like watching poetry in motion. He was efficient and methodical, like a well-oiled machine. He alternated time between the free weights and various machines, and by the time he'd finished, he'd been hot and sweaty, every muscle pumped and in beautiful form. Audrey sighed and bit her lip, remembering.

Ordinarily hot and sweaty didn't do it for her, but the entire time she'd watched him, she'd been muddled and warm, and hit with the inexplicable urge to lick him all over. The side of his neck, the V between his shoulder blades. She wanted to taste his skin, feel those muscles play beneath her fingertips. He might have been the one to work up a sweat, but she'd been the one on fire.

He knew it, too, the cocky jerk.

To her immense mortification, he'd caught her staring at him too often to even consider trying to be anything but a total wreck. He'd grinned, the wretch, then had pinned her to a mirror when no one was looking and kissed the hell out of her.

It was at that point that Audrey had come to a decision. Tewanda was right—she *did* want him. More than she'd ever wanted anybody and with an intensity that shook her to the very core. And Carlos had been right as well—what had being cautious ever done for her? Her entire life had been about helping others, pleasing others. With the exception of going to the college of her choosing and ultimately taking a risk on Unwind, what had she ever done strictly for herself? The answer was sobering.

Nothing.

She could list a dozen reasons she shouldn't sleep with Jamie—her grandfather's relationship with him, for starters. Not to mention Derrick, who would *not* get the answer he wanted from her this weekend. Even if he didn't follow through with his threat to break things off with her, she'd already decided that she'd end the relationship herself. It was a dead end. She didn't love him. Staying with him because he was safe—because he didn't make her feel anything—was a disservice to him and to herself.

Yes, there were a lot of legitimate reasons she shouldn't sleep with Jamie, and only one reason she should…and that was the one she was going with.

She wanted him.

He was the puppy in the window, the candy through the glass, the last piece of cake on the platter. He was every risk she'd never taken, every thanks-but-no-thanks, every missed opportunity.

But more importantly, tonight he was hers.

Moses lifted his head from her lap, signaling Jamie's timely arrival. The dog murmured a low woof, then lumbered off the sofa to the door. Audrey stood, felt a wild thrill whip through her midsection and her palms suddenly tingled in anticipation of what was to come. She grabbed Moses by the collar and opened the door.

Jamie smiled, a crooked sexy grin that made her heart do an odd little dance. He'd loaded the testicle basket with the bottle of whiskey and a bouquet of flowers he'd obviously snagged from the landscaping beds. Odd that she'd find that endearing. "For you," he said, offering it to her.

Chuckling, Audrey accepted the gift. "Come in," she told him. She gestured toward his gift. "Nice to see you found a purpose for your basket."

Jamie sidled forward, brushed his lips across hers and nuzzled her cheek. "I'm nothing if not resourceful."

Heaven help her, Audrey thought, because her heart was nothing if not doomed.

JAMIE HAD BARELY TAKEN A STEP into the room before Moses had once again gone for his crotch. He grunted, made a little "whoa-ho-ho" noise, and stepped back, awkwardly trying to avoid being victimized by the dog again. Honestly, he knew this was normal canine behavior, but couldn't help being embarrassed nonetheless. This was the third time, dammit. It was beginning to become a habit. "*Moses,* please, man," he said with a shaky laugh. "I don't know you well enough and, even if I did, you aren't my type."

Audrey's face pinkened and she hurriedly dragged the dog back once more, no small feat when the animal had to weigh in excess of 150 pounds. "Moses," she admonished through gritted teeth. *"Cut it out."* She pushed a hand through her long curly hair. "I've got a solution for this," she said. "Hold on." She disappeared into the kitchen, then returned a few seconds later with an aerosol can. "This won't stain," she told him, and before he knew what she was about to do, she aimed the can at his crotch and sprayed him with it. Jamie gaped. "What the—"

"Turn around."

"What?"

"Turn around," she repeated. "I need to put a shot of this on your—"

"Ass," he supplied helpfully. Jamie wrinkled his nose. "What is that? It smells."

"Exactly. It's a repellent." She stood once more, popped the lid back on the can. "It'll keep him from, you know—" she gestured toward his package "—checking you out."

Now this was a first, Jamie thought, absolutely stunned. He'd never had a *repellent* spayed upon his privates. He felt a slow grin tug at the corner of his mouth. "This only works on the dog, right?"

She laughed, the sound feminine and oddly gentle. "Right. I use it to keep him out of things I don't want him messing with."

Did that mean she wanted exclusive rights to his penis? Jamie wondered, resisting the urge to tease her further about it.

Seemingly following his line of thinking, she darted him a somewhat sheepish look. "Well, you know what I mean."

God, she was beautiful. Jamie grinned. "I do."

She turned and started back toward the kitchen. "I hope you like Italian."

Unexpected delight expanded in his chest. "You cooked for me?"

"Baked ziti," she said, neatly avoiding his question. "Caesar salad and chocolate pie for dessert."

"Sounds fabulous. You didn't have to go to all that trouble," he told her, and he meant it. In fact, though he appreciated the gesture, it made him feel downright uncomfortable knowing that he planned to use the massage as a seduction tool. He'd brought that bottle of whiskey, a bouquet of flowers and a handful of rubbers just to mark the occasion.

And she'd been busy cooking for him.

Though he knew it was ridiculous, her gesture pleased him far more than it should have. His mother and grandmother cooked for him all the time when he'd been at home and he'd had one serious girlfriend in college—Shelley-the-two-timing-bitch-Edwards—who'd cooked for him while they'd lived together. Since then, he hadn't gotten close enough to a woman to warrant something as domestic as cooking. This was nice, Jamie decided, inexplicably pleased.

"Make yourself at home," Audrey called. "I've got to pull this out of the oven."

"Can I help?"

"No, I've got it, thanks."

Rather than park himself on her sofa, Jamie wandered around her living room, inspecting various pictures which lined her mantel. Not surprisingly, there were several of her and the Colonel. A couple of candid shots of her down by the lake. Several chronicled Moses's growth, Jamie noted, resulting in a smile. Proud momma, eh? he thought with a shake of his head. Interestingly enough, there were no pictures of Derrick. He grimaced with pleasure and rocked back on his heels.

That had to be significant.

As for her house, it was a larger version of the cottages. White beadboard lined the bottom of the walls and she'd painted the top an interesting shade of blue, the color of an almost-but-not-quite night sky. Various vintage prints—Art Deco— were scattered around the room and a large antique mirror hung over her fireplace.

A comfy contemporary sofa had been dressed up with puffy floral pillows and instead of a traditional coffee table, she'd opted for an old seaman's trunk. It was an eclectic mix of old and new—the end result was not only a reflection of herself, but comfortable and homey as well. He could very easily see her and Moses curled up on her couch watching TV and snacking, and to his acute discomfort, his imagination obligingly Photoshopped himself into that picture.

Audrey chose that moment to peer around the kitchen wall. "Dinner's on," she said, smiling. That adorable dimple winked in her cheek.

Once again, he was struck by just how beautiful she really was. Something in his chest squeezed, almost painfully. She'd left her espresso curls down and loose and, if she wore any make-up aside from a coat of pinkish gloss on her lips, she'd applied it with a very light hand. She was fresh and open and those kind, soothing eyes twinkled with some sort of hidden joy. She was bright and infectious and sexy as hell—the total package. Jamie released a pent-up breath, one he hadn't realized he'd been holding. And the Colonel was right, he thought.

She *was* special.

And there was no way in hell he was going to let her marry Derrick.

Seduction on, he thought, purposely kicking the charm factor up a notch. Playtime was over.

_10_

AUDREY WATCHED Jamie's lips curl into that trademark bone-melting grin as he sidled into her kitchen, and she felt the abrupt shift in his intent. It was as though he'd flipped a switch, the change was so remarkable.

He wore a pair of faded denim jeans which were tight in all the right places and a brown cable-knit sweater which accentuated his broad, muscled shoulders and picked up the golden tones of those remarkably sexy eyes. From the looks of things, he'd attempted to gel his unruly curls into place, but had failed because they'd sprung free, a riot of loose and sexy locks she simply itched to push her fingers through. He obligingly pulled her chair out for her.

"Thank you," Audrey murmured.

"You're welcome," he said silkily. He took his own seat. "Thank you for cooking. It's been a long time since I've had a home-cooked meal."

"Oh?" Fishing again, but what the hell? By this point he should expect it. Audrey filled his salad bowl first, then hers.

He grinned and his gaze twinkled with knowing humor. "You never give up, do you?"

She speared a forkful and shot him a smile. "No. It's part of my charm."

"Oh, I don't think I'd say that," Jamie told her, his gaze dropping with lingering accuracy to her lips. He finally relented with a sigh. "Let's just say that I have a roommate who isn't any better in the kitchen than I am, and my mother and grandmother live too far away to make dropping by their house for dinner do-able."

"How far out of Atlanta do they live?"

Jamie finished a bite of salad. "Five and half hours. They're in Alabama."

So that was the Roll Tide connection. Her grandfather had told her that they'd met at the University of Alabama. She should have realized that he still had family there.

In the process of carefully moving all of his olives to the side of his plate, Audrey frowned. "You don't like olives. I'm sorry," she said. "I should have asked."

Jamie glanced up. "No problem," he assured

her with an easier grin. "They're easy to spot and easy to move."

"And—" Audrey forked one up from the side of his plate "—they are not meant to go to waste. I *love* olives."

Jamie stilled for a fraction of a second, watched the olive leave his plate via her fork and then land in her mouth. Audrey swallowed. "Is something wrong?" she asked. Maybe he didn't like them on salad, but preferred them otherwise? "Were you going to eat that?"

"No," he said, blinking out of whatever had bothered him. He made a face. "Olives are nasty. They're not in the ziti, are they?"

Audrey chuckled. "No."

Jamie ladled some of the Italian dish onto her plate, then his. "Good." He paused. "You know, if we were dating, this would be like our…third date, wouldn't it?"

The question came so far out of left field that Audrey choked on her wine. "Uh… Well, we aren't dating, so it's a moot point. But yeah, I suppose if we were, this would be considered our third date of sorts." Bewildered, she darted him a confused glance. "Why do you ask?"

"No reason," he said quickly, then shoved a

forkful of ziti into his mouth. He looked curiously alarmed, though for the life of her, she couldn't imagine why.

Audrey frowned. "Are you all right? You look a little flushed."

"This is spicy."

No, it wasn't, Audrey thought, thoroughly baffled by his behavior. Rather than pursue it, though, she decided to continue their conversation. He'd finally given her a little bit of personal information. That was a start, at any rate.

"So your family lives too far away to cook for you. What about a girlfriend? There's no future Mrs. Flanagan wannabe who whips up meals in your honor?"

The comment drew a laugh, full and throaty, and seemed to ground him once more. He picked up his glass, inspected the contents. "Er. No."

Audrey shrugged, ridiculously pleased. Honestly, she had no vested interest in whether or not he had a girlfriend, but she couldn't deny that the idea that there might be another woman in his life irritated her beyond prudent reason. In fact, it made her downright ill. A significant revelation no doubt lurked in her disproportionate jealousy, but why ruin what was going to be a wonderful evening with expectations and what-might-have-beens?

"What about you?" Jamie asked, turning the probing conversation around on her. "Does the future Mr. Audrey Kincaid cook for you?" he drawled.

She grimaced, smiled. "There is no future Mr. Audrey Kincaid."

His gaze tangled with hers above the rim of his glass. "But I thought you said you were supposed to be considering a marriage proposal this week?"

She cocked her head, conceding the point. "I am. I've considered. I'm saying no."

Though she might have imagined it, something seemed to shift in Jamie's gaze. He hadn't moved, hadn't so much as blinked, and yet she felt him tune in more fully. "Really? What made you come to that conclusion?"

A laugh broke up in her throat and she rolled her eyes. "You mean aside from the fact that I can't keep myself from kissing you?" she said, grinning. "He's just not the man for me. It, uh… It wouldn't be fair to either of us."

"Would you have said no if you had been able to resist kissing me?" he asked, looking entirely too pleased with himself.

"No, I'd planned to say no all along." She scooted a cut glass tumbler toward him and gestured toward the Jameson. "I was just dreading it."

Jamie's eyes twinkled with some sort of secret humor. He poured her a shot of the whiskey and slid it back to her, then hefted his own glass. "Here you go," he said. "Liquid courage."

How timely, Audrey thought, as she brought the tumbler to her lips. She was going to need it because she grimly suspected he planned to call in his massage any minute now. *Her hands on that hot silky skin, shaping those incredible muscles...* She took a drink, allowed the smooth honey-like taste of the whiskey to caress her tongue before swallowing. He was right, she thought, immeasurably pleased—no burn. Just a pleasant warmth which quickly expanded in her belly, then gradually infected the rest of her body.

Audrey inclined her head. "This is good," she told him.

Jamie shrugged. "I like it."

"Are you ready for dessert?" she asked.

His sexy twinkling gaze told her he had other ideas in mind. "Maybe later," Jamie said. He leaned back in his chair and absently scratched his chest. "I thought I'd let you go ahead and give me that massage."

Audrey chuckled. "*Let* me, eh? How thoughtful of you," she said wryly.

"I'm nothing if not thoughtful."

"I thought you said you were nothing if not resourceful?"

Jamie nodded sanctimoniously. "That, too."

Audrey laughed, then stood and cleared their plates. "You're nothing if not full of shit, that's what you are."

"Let me help you," Jamie offered, chuckling. He stood and quickly helped her clear the table. It was nice, Audrey decided, warmed from a combination of his presence and the Jameson.

When the last dish was washed and dried, she took a deep breath, and then turned to face him. "Thank you," she said, feeling uncharacteristically sheepish.

Jamie nodded, pressing a shameless hand against his chest. "What can I say? I'm nothing if not helpful."

Actually, he was nothing if not gorgeous and charming and wonderful and she wanted him more with each passing second. Her gaze tangled with his and the breath seemed to thin in her lungs.

A hot cocktail of seduction and sex was imminent. She could feel it every time that somnolent gaze raked over her. Her skin prickled and her belly fluttered with unstable air. She was a wreck, Audrey decided. A sexually frustrated wreck.

"Where do you want me?" Jamie asked.

Audrey blinked. "What?"

He laughed, the sound intimate and darkly sexy. "For my massage," he explained.

Well, they could save a lot of time by merely moving things to her bedroom, but she supposed she should at least give the impression of not being a complete pushover and administer the massage in the living room on her massage table.

"I, uh…" She jerked her finger toward the other room. "I'll just go set it up."

"Audrey?"

She turned on her heel, but before she could take a single step, Jamie stopped her with a mere touch of his hand.

"Yes?"

"You don't have to do this if you don't want to," he said softly, the comment rife with double meaning. Though the smile was the same charming grin he always wore, there was a sweet sincerity in his gaze which made her silly heart melt like a pat of butter over a hot bun. He was giving her an out, a get-out-of-sex free card.

The trouble was…she didn't want one.

The first time he'd kissed her, he'd asked permission, but she wasn't gentleman enough to give him any such courtesy. Audrey leaned forward, wrapped her arms around his neck and laid a kiss on him she knew would dispel any doubts about what she wanted or her intentions. "Come on," she finally told him. "It's time for me to work some of those kinks out for you."

A wicked chuckle rumbled up his throat. "Be gentle."

"Oh, believe me," she assured him. "I'm nothing if not gentle."

FOR THE FIRST TIME in his life Jamie was stuck with a true moral dilemma. To seduce or not seduce? Technically, since she had no intention of marrying Derrick, he could dub this mission successful and go home. He'd be free, Jamie realized. He would have paid his debt to the Colonel, could officially cut ties with his past and move forward. That was the lie he'd been propagating, at any rate. There was nothing to gain for his so-called cause if he seduced her.

And yet for reasons he didn't dare explore, he knew—*knew*—that *he* had everything to gain… and even more to lose if he didn't.

Besides, the first touch of her cool fingers against his back set a path into motion he didn't have a prayer of changing. It would have been like trying to route a detour in the middle of a bridge—pointless.

"Remind me to thank Tewanda," Jamie told her, his voice low and rusty to his own ears.

Audrey chuckled softly, kneading the muscles in his shoulders with small, competent, surprisingly strong hands. "Me, too," Audrey said. "Though I wanted to throttle her when she first suggested this."

"Really?" Jamie asked. "You mean speaking through gritted teeth isn't how you normally express excitement and joy?" he teased, remembering her murderous expression that first night in the lodge.

She laughed, skimmed her nails down his spine, eliciting a shiver of delight. "Noticed that, did you?"

He grunted wryly. "It was hard to miss."

"And yet you wouldn't let it go," Audrey added. "I wonder why," she mused aloud, her conversational tone rife with exaggerated humor.

Jamie felt another laugh rattle his belly. "I would think it would be obvious. I wanted your hands on my body," he murmured softly. "Like they are now."

He heard a stuttering breath leak out of her lungs, felt her touch grow a little bolder. She rubbed and kneaded, methodically working his muscles until they were melting under her exquisite touch. Meanwhile another muscle below his waistline was anything but melting. He felt her fingers trace an inverted heart, then linger and outline the tattoo on his right shoulder blade.

Sonofabitch, Jamie thought, involuntarily tensing. He squeezed his eyes tightly shut, braced himself, knowing she would ask. And knowing that he was in no shape to resist.

"Oh." She sighed softly, her heart in her voice. "Who was Danny?"

A fist of pain tightened in Jamie's chest. Unbidden images from that horrible night flashed like a broken projector through his brain. He tried to stop it, tried to push it away, but failed.

Danny's bloodstained chest, a huge gaping wound littered with torn cloth and sand. "Leave me, dammit! Leave me! You know it's over!"

Panic, fear and adrenaline rushed through

Jamie's bloodstream, making Danny's 240-plus pound body feel virtually weightless. Jamie's heart threatened to pound right out of his chest and the urge to weep was almost more than he could bear. He had to get Danny to the truck—if he could only get him to the truck, they'd be safe. He almost tripped. Righted himself. Kept going. "It's not over until I say it's over."

Bullets whizzed by, spraying up sand. "God-dammit, Jamie! Leave me. There's no p-point in us both d-dying out here."

"I won't leave you," Jamie had growled, running until his lungs had burned and he'd had to swallow the urge to retch. Then he'd looked down into his friend's pale blood-speckled face and told the biggest lie of his life. "You aren't going to die, dammit. I've got you. Just hang on."

"Jamie?"

Audrey's soft voice penetrated the waking nightmare.

"Are you okay?" she asked, her fingers still hovering over his tattoo, his memorial to a fallen friend—an eagle with a ribbon and the inscription "In Memory of Danny Boy" trailing from its beak.

No, he wasn't okay. He would never be okay. He'd failed to keep his friend's back. It was his fault Danny'd been hit and his fault that he hadn't gotten him to safety.

He was a murderer by default and nothing would ever change that.

"Oh, Jamie," she said, bending down to kiss his back. "Give it to me and let me help you," she implored softly. "Tell me about Danny."

For one blind horrifying instant he was struck with the impulse to do just that. That was her specialty, after all. Taking damaged people and fixing them. If he opened himself up to her, could she heal him? Jamie wondered. Could she mend the yawning hole in his soul? For whatever reason, he knew if there was a person on the planet who could do just that, it was her. Jamie swallowed. Being with Audrey, something as simple as sharing the same air, made him feel more human and more alive than he had in months.

Unfortunately he wasn't worthy of healing—he didn't deserve it—and even more importantly, he wouldn't become one of those "life-suckers" who drained her that the Colonel had told him about.

He wouldn't become her next pity project, dammit.

"Look, Jamie, I know this is hard, but sometimes talking about things—"

Enough already.

Before she could finish the sentence, Jamie turned over, rolled into a sitting position and pulled her into the open V between his thighs. Time to shut her up before he did something stupid, like spill his guts and cry. "No more talking," he told her.

Then he fitted his mouth to hers and kissed her until he felt every bit of the resistance melt from her body and felt a new kind of tension—the right kind—take its place. Ah, he thought, the panic lessening. Familiar ground.

She parlayed every bold thrust of his tongue and pushed her hands into his hair. A little sigh of pleasure leaked from her mouth into his and there was something so inherently erotic about that telling breath that he felt as though his chest and dick were both going to explode before he could get himself inside her.

Her long curls trickled over his shoulder, framed them in a world of their own making, one where nothing existed outside the meeting of their mouths and the inevitable joining of their bodies.

Jamie slid his hands down her back, found the hem of her shirt and tugged. One touch of his fingers against her soft bare skin made his penis jerk hard in his shorts. Oh, God, she was so perfect she made him ache. Supple and womanly, her scent an intriguing mixture of apple and spice— wholesomely wicked. He wanted to be gentle, wanted to prime her, make her so blind with need that she'd never imagine sharing her goodness with another man, and yet now that the time was upon them, Jamie didn't have the strength to hold back.

And it was equally—*gratifyingly*—obvious that she didn't either.

Her touch was sure, but impatient, her greedy palms sliding all over him, blazing a tingly trail of heat everywhere that she touched him. And she had the advantage because he was already half-naked, while she on the other hand was still fully clothed. That definitely needed rectifying, Jamie thought, setting himself to the task. He pulled her shirt up over her head, tossed it aside.

Creamy skin, lacy pale pink bra, tiny waist.

God help him.

He groaned, pulled her to him and licked a path over the rim of each cup, sampled the delectable spill-over flesh. His hands framed the small of her back, then pushed her pants down and over the sweet swell of her rump.

Matching thong, barely the size of a postage

stamp. Equally lacy and sheer, with a butterfly hovering expectantly over her dark curls. Looking for nectar, no doubt, Jamie thought with a wicked chuckle, as every bit of the blood in his body suddenly gathered in his loins. His lips curled. He imagined he'd be more successful than the butter-fly.

He fingered the lace riding high on her hip. "Nice," he murmured.

Audrey smiled. "Glad you approve." She slid a hand down the front of his boxers, boldly cupped him through the fabric, causing a hiss of air to push past his teeth. "This is nice as well."

A strangled laugh bubbled up his throat. "And I'm glad you approve."

"I'd approve even more if you'd put it to better use," she said, giving him a gentle squeeze.

Shocked, another chuckle vibrated his belly. "As you wish," Jamie told her. He punctuated the promise with a deft flick of his fingers which made her bra pop open, revealing her pert, lush breasts. Rosy nipples puckered, seemingly in waiting for his kiss. He bent his head and pulled one perfect peak into his mouth, suckled her soft, then hard, flattening the bud against the roof of his mouth.

Audrey whimpered, grasped his shoulders, her nails biting into his flesh. She moved closer to him, lightly skimmed a hand over his chest, down his belly and beneath the waistband of his shorts. Then she was touching him and everything else simply faded into a blur of frantic—frenetic—sexual energy. The incessant need, the drive, was stronger than anything he'd ever experienced and, he instinctively knew, ever would again.

His dick practically leaped into her hand, anxious for her touch. She worked the slippery skin up and down his shaft, nipped at his shoulder while he moved to her other breast. Kneading, sucking, licking. He wanted to taste her all over. Couldn't get enough of her. Fire licked through his veins and into hers. She was a fever inside him, an itch he couldn't scratch.

"I want you so damned bad," Jamie told her. He brushed his fingers past her butterfly and smiled against her neck when they came back wet.

"Then take me," she taunted, running a finger over his engorged head. She wriggled out of her panties.

A second later he'd located a condom, another three and he was ready. He whirled her around, sat her on the edge of the massage table, then spread her legs and in one solid thrust, pushed into her. Her breath caught in her throat, her lids fluttered closed and her head dropped back, seemingly too heavy for her neck.

Interminable seconds passed as Jamie absorbed the feel of her around him. His heart segued into an irregular rhythm, his legs shook, and he had to lock his jaw to keep from roaring in primal, almost caveman-like approval. Every hair on his body prickled with awareness and his stomach did a little pirouette of pleasure. Nothing in his past experience could have prepared him for the complete *rightness* of this moment. Everything began and ended here, Jamie thought, shaken—re-formed and reborn—to the very core.

He looked down at her, bare breasts, sweet belly, his rod buried into her warmth, then his gaze tangled with hers—soothing and blue and heartbreakingly beautiful—and James Aidan Flanagan did the one thing he'd sworn he'd never do.

He fell head over heels in love.

11

IT TOOK EVERY OUNCE of willpower Audrey possessed not to pass out. The feel of Jamie's body inside her—the desperate need in his eyes—was so intense it literally took her breath away.

So far, she hadn't been able to get it back.

He was big and solid and his presence consumed her. And those gorgeous hazel eyes… Tortured, anguished, wondering, wistful and curiously doomed. She didn't have to be psychic to know what he was thinking.

She could *feel* it.

He wanted her, but didn't want to. He needed her help, but would never willingly accept it. He was hurting and angry and bitter and hopeless.

She'd felt those emotions and more when she'd touched his tattoo, a permanent tribute to a man who'd given the ultimate sacrifice for his country. Naturally when she'd pressed for more information, he'd derailed her with sex. A blatant stall tactic, but how could she complain when he felt so right seated between her legs?

Audrey tightened around him, drew him even farther into her body. She watched the veins in his neck strain, watched him lock his jaw and a thrill of feminine power whipped through her, urging her to take even more. She angled her hips forward, pushing him even deeper inside her and saw little stars dance in her peripheral vision.

God, he felt good. Better than anything she could have ever imagined.

Jamie withdrew, then plunged back in sending shock waves of sexual delight pulsing through her. Her womb contracted, slickening her folds. They'd barely started and yet, amazingly, she could already feel the quickening of climax tingling in her clit. This felt so right and it had been so very long—*so very, very long*—since she'd had a proper orgasm, she couldn't bear to wait a second longer. She wanted to savor it, but couldn't summon the strength. She worked herself beneath him, forcing him to up the tempo to give her more.

Jamie answered with a wicked chuckle, wrapped a muscled arm around her waist and pounded into her. He was hot, hard and thrilling.

Harder, harder, then faster and faster still. Deep then shallow, a fabulous combination designed to energize every nerve inside of her. She was coming apart, Audrey decided, as the tension inside her wound tighter and tighter. Any second now she was simply going to break and fly into a million pieces.

Jamie bent forward, licked a wild path over both nipples, then sucked one into the hot cavern of his mouth.

She fractured.

Her back bowed so hard off the massage table she feared it would break, her mouth opened in a silent scream and she dug her nails into his ass, holding him there while she convulsed around him. Every contraction around the hot, hard length of him made her limbs weaken. The orgasm tore through her, whipped her insides into an erupting volcano of sensation so perfect it brought tears to her eyes.

The force of her own release triggered Jamie's. His lips peeled away from his teeth and a feral growl of approval, which would have made a caveman proud, ripped from his throat. He lodged himself firmly into her, so tight and so deep you couldn't have gotten a toothpick between them.

It was more than just an orgasm, Audrey realized as her gaze tangled with his, it was a statement.

She was his. He'd claimed her.

For all intents and purposes, he'd just planted a no trespassing sign in her vagina. It was barbaric and romantic and her idiot heart soared with ridiculous joy. Chest heaving, she let her head fall back and a long peal of glorious laughter echoed up her throat.

Evidently pleased with himself, Jamie bent and kissed her forehead. "You look happy."

"What tipped you off? The smile or the orgasm?"

He chuckled, carefully withdrew, then helped her up, thank God, because she couldn't have managed it on her own strength. "Both." He cocked his head toward the back of her house. "Are you up for a little lather-rinse-repeat?" he asked.

Another dark thrill coursed through her. "You want to take a shower?"

His voice lowered an octave. "Among other things."

Ooh-la-la, Audrey thought as, unbelievably, her womb issued another greedy contraction. That must be where the "repeat" part came in. *Jamie, naked, wet, needy and hard...*

Oh, yeah. She could definitely go for that. Among other things.

HE'D DONE IT, Jamie thought. After a lifetime of being very careful—of always maintaining an emotional distance—in the course of the past four days he'd abandoned and broken every bachelor rule. He and Audrey had had more than three unofficial dates. She'd eaten off his plate. And, he thought, as his gaze traced the beautiful lines of her slumbering face, he'd spent the night with her.

In her bed, no less.

Strangely enough, no clap of thunder rent the heavens and the first rays of dawn peeking above the horizon didn't appear any different from any other he'd witnessed in his thirty-some-odd years on this earth.

And yet everything had changed.

Not in the world around him, Jamie thought. No, she'd changed his world from *within*. The world he lived in might not have changed, but the one inside him no longer remotely resembled the one he'd been a part of before.

Somehow, someway, when he hadn't been paying attention, he'd fallen in love with her. He wouldn't have knowingly done it—he was too much of a coward—but he couldn't deny that it had happened nonetheless. And never had that been more startlingly clear than when he'd pushed into her and looked into those calm clear blue eyes. She'd been so perfect that he'd felt the back of his lids burn with some unnamed emotion he hadn't had the courage to claim in years.

No doubt, he'd become the butt of his friends' jokes—oh, how the mighty have fallen, they'd tease—and Garrett would most likely make good on his threat, but this morning, in this very instant, frankly he just didn't give a damn.

So long as he was with her, the rest of the world could simply go to hell.

He wasn't going to worry about Garrett or what he would say. He wasn't going to worry about his role in meddling in her private business. He wasn't going to worry about falling in love and the resulting powerlessness that would no doubt bring. He just wanted to be with her.

Audrey's head was on his shoulder, her sweet hand curled palm down against his chest—his heart, specifically—and he could feel her plump breast resting against his side. Moses lay sprawled at the foot of the bed—on his feet, thank you very much—and from his vantage point beside the window, Jamie could see a couple of squirrels leaping from tree to tree. Their antics drew a smile. He felt Audrey stir and turned to watch her wake.

Her eyes were heavy-lidded with the last vestiges of sleep. She caught him watching her, smiled sleepily, then stretched like a cat. "Goodmorning," she murmured groggily.

"Morning, beautiful," Jamie told her.

"I'm glad you stayed. I'd pegged you for the leaving type."

In another life, with any other woman—but not with her. His gaze tangled with hers. "You're worth waking up with."

She smiled at the compliment and a stain of pink washed over her cheeks. Amazing, Jamie thought. He'd taken her six ways to Sunday last night—on the massage table, in her shower, against the hall wall and in her bed…and yet she couldn't take a compliment from him without blushing. Odd that he should find that endearing.

"So are you." She reached up and tousled his hair. "Your curls are all mussed."

"So are yours."

She grimaced. "But yours are sexy, whereas mine look like they've been hit with a weedwhacker and styled with a garden rake."

"Not true," Jamie told her, fingering one long curl. He wrapped it around his index finger and tugged her toward him for a sweet kiss. "I love your hair. It makes me hot."

Another one of those nervous smiles. Intrigued, Jamie sat up on one elbow and stared at her. "Are you not accustomed to compliments, or do they just make you uncomfortable?"

"Both," Audrey told him.

He traced a finger down the achingly familiar slope of her cheek. "We'll have to work on that."

"You could stand a little work yourself," she told him, her gaze searching his.

Since he knew she was referring to his inability to open up, Jamie decided a subject change was in order. "We could stand to work on breakfast," he improvised. "Are you hungry?"

Though she clearly wrestled with pursuing the line of conversation she'd started, to Jamie's immense relief Audrey let it drop. Not permanently, he knew, but at least he'd gotten a reprieve. She nodded. "Yeah. Let me take Moses out, then I'll fix us something."

"Let me," Jamie offered. He pushed up and planted his feet on the floor. "You cooked last night."

"You don't have to do that," she said. "You don't know your way around my kitchen."

Jamie chuckled. "I think I can manage," he drawled, shooting her a wicked grin. For someone who was determined to help the world, she wasn't very good at accepting help herself, Jamie noted, intrigued.

Audrey chewed the corner of her lip and her eyes twinkled with humor. "Smart-ass."

"How about 'Thank you, Jamie, that sounds nice'?"

"Thank you, Jamie," she replied dutifully. "I like my eggs over medium and prefer strawberry jam on my toast."

Ah, now that was more like it. "What am I?" he teased. "Your short-order cook?"

Audrey stood, shrugged into her robe and shot him an unrepentant grin. "You asked for it."

What could he say to that? She was right.

"Come on, Moses," she said, her voice trailing off in a sigh. "Time to give your offering to Mother Earth." She paused, turned and shot him another smile. "And there's absolutely nothing *short* about you."

"Thank you," Jamie told her, feigning a humble nod. "*That's* how you take a compliment."

Rather than comment, Audrey merely shook her head and left. Though he dreaded it, Jamie waited until he heard the back door close, then checked the display on his cell phone. He cringed when he saw two missed calls—both were from the Colonel.

"Flanagan, I want an update. Give me a call back ASAP."

The second call was received at eleven-thirty and was a lot less cordial. "Flanagan, you'd better be taking a late-night basket-weaving lesson because if you are doing anything—*anything*—that you're not supposed to be doing with my granddaughter, I will be on the first available plane up there and will personally tear your nuts from your body. *Do not* toy with my granddaughter's affections."

Was it toying with her affections if he wanted to be the sole object of her affection? Jamie wondered. Didn't matter. He sincerely doubted that the Colonel would recognize the difference.

For a moment Jamie considered telling Audrey about the real reason for his visit. Given what they'd shared and everything he wanted to share in the future, it didn't seem right to keep it from her. She'd be pissed at first, of course, and he could hardly blame her, but she wasn't completely unreasonable. She'd recognize that her grandfather had only had her best interests at heart and that he'd merely been repaying a favor.

Ultimately, though, he decided against it. Audrey had never had any intention of shackling herself to that self-important blowhard, as the Colonel had put it. And she needn't ever know that anyone had interfered, least of all him. And this worked out nicely for him, as he wasn't altogether sure that she would see things the way that he wanted her to. Self-serving? Manipulative? Selfish?

Certainly.

But the end justified the means here, Jamie decided, because it would damned hard to love her properly if she hated him.

And the idea of Audrey hating him was…unthinkable. What were his plans? Aside from making her breakfast, then making love to her again, he didn't have any. But he knew that in any future plans he had, he wanted her in them.

"A-HA!"

In the process of coming around the corner of her house, Audrey started, swallowed a scream, then pressed a hand to her rapidly beating heart. "Tewanda, what the hell are you doing?" she snapped. "You scared the life out of me." She glared at Moses. "Some guard dog you are," she mumbled.

"I was waiting on you," Tewanda told her. "He's in there, isn't he? Stella got her groove back last night, eh?" she asked, her voice loaded with innuendo. She danced around in a little circle. "Uh-huh, uh-huh, uh-huh. I can tell. You've got the glow. The orgasm aura."

"Shut up," Audrey hissed, shooting a furtive look over her shoulder. "He'll hear you."

Tewanda sidled forward. "Well?" she asked pointedly, her eyes dancing with do-tell mischief.

"Well what?"

She let go an exasperated huff. *"How was it?"*

Audrey wanted to hold back, to make her audacious friend suffer, but ultimately she couldn't do it. She giggled—actually giggled. "It. Was. *Amazing.*"

Tewanda did her little dance again. "I knew it! Some guys you can just tell, you know, and the two of you were casting sparks from the get-go." She paused. "So what are you going to do about Derrick? Cutting him lose, right? Telling him no? Adios, sayonara, goodbye, don't let the door hit you on the ass on your way out?"

"Tewanda." Honestly, Audrey thought, stifling

the urge to laugh. She didn't know what had made her friend happier—that she'd finally had magnificent sex or that she was breaking up with Derrick.

"Well, you can't mean to stay with him, right?" Tewanda asked. She paused, considered her. "There's more here with Jamie already than there's ever been with Derrick. Hell, even I can see that."

She was right, Audrey knew. Four days into a relationship with Jamie had yielded more emotion than fourteen months with Derrick. Jamie did it for her on all levels. He was brilliant and funny, a bit wounded but not damaged beyond repair, though she knew he didn't believe that. He was loyal and gorgeous and…and she'd fallen for him, Audrey realized helplessly.

It was that simple and that complicated.

The idea that he was supposed to leave tomorrow made her previously happy heart constrict with panic. She didn't want him to leave. Ever, she thought with a wry twist of her lips, though that might be a tad premature.

All she knew was that she wanted him. She wanted to share every dawn and every sunset, every victory and every setback. She wanted to always see those laughing hazel eyes and bask in that crooked sexy grin. She wanted more lather, rinse and repeat, Audrey thought with a small grin as her insides did another little meltdown.

But most importantly, she wanted to help him. She was close, she knew. She could tell they were teetering on the edge of a breakthrough. Meaning that she'd just about pushed him to the breaking point and every bit of that pent-up grief, regret and misplaced guilt was going to come boiling to the surface. He'd come dangerously close last night and, while she could have pushed this morning, intuition had told her to hold back.

Though he'd derailed her with sex last night, she didn't want anything coming between them in bed. Bed needed to be a safe zone, Audrey thought. For whatever reason, she got the distinct impression that it hadn't been for Jamie. That he rarely, if ever, lingered for any intimacy.

Moses did his business, then trotted back to her side.

"So what now?" Tewanda asked. "Are you still sticking to the schedule or are you going to improvise?"

They were supposed to start ballroom dancing this morning, but given the time factor Audrey had working against her, she decided that adhering to the schedule wasn't a good idea. "We're improvising," she said.

Tewanda clearly took that as doublespeak for sex-all-day. "No worries," she said, smiling like a Cheshire cat. "Turn the walkie off. There's nothing here that can't go without your attention for one day. Go commando and incommunicado and get laid-o." She whooped joyously again, then started back toward the office.

Smiling, Audrey merely shook her head.

Tewanda paused, turned and shot her a look which was curiously serious and sincere for a person who'd only a moment ago told her to get laid-o, for pity's sake. "Audrey?"

"Yeah?"

"I'm happy for you. He's a good thing."

Audrey's chest warmed and a small smile tugged at her lips. "Yeah," she agreed, nodding. "He is."

And a girl could never have too much of a good thing.

12

Now, HE COULD TRULY get used to this, Jamie thought contentedly. He and Audrey had said to hell with the schedule, she'd turned off her walkie-talkie and they'd spent the entire day doing whatever struck their fancy. He'd made breakfast, they'd eaten, then showered, then enjoyed another session of lather, rinse and repeat. His lips quirked.

Equally as frantic as last night—he couldn't get into her fast enough—but somehow more intense than before. In fact, every moment he spent with her seemed to be more powerful than the last. And yet she was easy company. He felt…complete in her presence. Go figure?

At the moment he was resting with his head in her lap while she rowed them around the lake. It was late afternoon and the sun melted like a big scoop of orange sherbet above the trees, painting their riotous fall foliage in fiery color. It was truly beautiful here, Jamie thought, dragging in a breath of cool crisp air. Though he'd lived all over the world, he'd always considered Alabama his home. But he could easily see making this his home as well.

Anywhere with her would be home, he realized, a bit startled by the epiphany.

The water lapped against the hull of the boat, birds sang and a gentle breeze whispered through the tops of the trees. Unwind was right, he thought, feeling his lids flutter shut.

Audrey's fingers skimmed his eyebrow, making a smile tug at his lips. "You look relaxed."

"I am," he said. "I like it here."

"You mean you like having your head in my lap or you like being at Unwind?"

He looked up at her. "Can I like both?"

She chuckled, the sound soft and intimate between them. "Certainly. I like them both as well."

Jamie frowned as a thought struck, a question he'd been meaning to ask but had kept forgetting. "You said you'd been a commodities broker in a past life," Jamie reminded her. "But you never told me how you ended up here."

She pretended she didn't know what he was talking about, the little nimrod. "Did you ask?"

"I did," Jamie confirmed, laughing. "You said if you told me that, you'd have to kill me. Permission granted. After you have satisfied my curiosity, you can take your best shot." It's not like she hadn't been taking shots at him all week. It wouldn't hurt her to reciprocate the gesture.

"It's not pretty," Audrey warned him.

"The truth rarely is. Come on. Tell me."

He heard her sigh, looked up and watched her gaze cloud over. "I had a heart attack," she said glibly, shrugging. "Stress. It was either lose the job or lose my life."

Jamie had to clamp his jaw to keep it from sagging. Out of all the reasons she could have listed as to why she'd made such an abrupt career change, a heart attack certainly would never have occurred to him.

Stunned, he sat up and turned around to face her. "But— But you're young. You're healthy." He frowned, gestured toward her chest. "How did—"

"A body can only take so much," she said, smiling sadly. "I put mine through hell. I was also with a guy who—" she paused, chose her words carefully "—required more of me than I could give. That relationship ended with a restraining order." She frowned with regret. "Not one of my better decisions, but we all have some we aren't proud of."

Jamie swore. He passed a hand over his face and his gaze inexplicably zeroed in once again on her chest. He got it, all right. The guy she'd been with had taken so much of her that he'd literally broken her heart. Not in the traditional sense, no, but damaged her all the same.

Christ. No wonder the Colonel had kept going on and on about how special she was. He'd known it, of course. A man couldn't spend half a second in her presence without feeling the healing, soul-soothing effects of her company. And hell, he'd even felt it from a friggin' picture, two thousand miles away from here. *A heart attack*, Jamie thought again, absolutely shaken.

"How are you doing now?" he asked quietly. "Taking meds? Watching your cholesterol?" Another thought struck. Surely to God all the wild sex they'd had in the past couple of days couldn't be good for her. The exertion, the orgasms… He could have killed her, Jamie thought, his own heart turning to lead and plummeting into his stomach. Sweet mother of—

Audrey chuckled. "I can see that your imagination is running away with you," she told him. "No, I am not on any medication, though I do watch my diet since I'll always be at risk." A small smile turned her lips. "And, for the record, there are no special limitations on my…physical activities you should concern yourself with."

"But—"

"I'm fine," Audrey insisted. "I take care of myself. I know it sounds like a big deal, but it really isn't."

The hell it wasn't, Jamie thought. "How old were you?"

"At the time it happened? Twenty-six."

"Then it was a big deal," Jamie said. Honestly, he'd heard of athletes who'd pushed themselves into a premature heart attack, but never a young healthy woman. The Colonel must have been out of his mind.

"Anyway," she said, releasing an end-of-subject sigh, one he recognized because he'd used it frequently himself. "That's how I got here. Who better to help stressed-out professionals than a former stressed-out professional, eh?"

He could certainly understand that, and there was no doubt she was in her element here. Still… "Do you miss your old job? Your old life?"

She smiled again, marginally lightening the load in his chest. "Not at all. I'm where I'm supposed to be. Everything happens for a reason." Her clear blue gaze tangled with his and a secret knowledge seemed to lurk there that he sincerely wished he was privy to. "You're here for a reason, too," she told him.

While he could have just as easily made a joke, Jamie didn't. "Do you really believe that?" he asked. "Or is that just a platitude people bandy about when they don't have an answer for something? It all comes down to fate," he said, a hint of bitterness he couldn't control seeping into his voice.

Audrey mulled it over, then ultimately nodded. "I think so. There's a point and purpose to everything. Just look at the way the world is designed. Even nature has a point, a goal, an end."

While he couldn't fault her reasoning, he couldn't accept it either. Accepting it meant that Danny had been destined to die on that hill, and that Jamie had been destined to fail when it had come to saving him. Fate? he scoffed. Then fate was an unfair bitch. He was bitter and angry and wanted to know why. *Why, dammit?* What possible good had come out of his friend losing his life?

Geez, God, he was losing it here. Until the past few days Jamie had done an admirable job of keeping a tight rein on his feelings. He'd put every ounce of grief, regret and anger into a neat box at the bottom of his soul and, while he'd suffer an occasional setback—nightmares, mostly—for the most part, he could go into lock-down mode and keep it together.

It was her, he realized. She was acting like a sponge, drawing to the surface everything inside him he wanted to keep hidden.

Audrey set the oars aside, leaned forward, framed his face and gave him a tender kiss. "I just gave you a painful piece of my history. Now I'm asking for one of yours. Tell me about Danny," she implored softly.

Jamie instinctively drew back, shut down. He knew what she was doing—she was trying to fix him, but there were some things that simply couldn't be fixed and he was one of them. She'd been doing this all week—picking, probing, question after question, trying to open him up and lay him bare. The mere thought turned his insides to ice, made bile rise in his throat.

"Leave it," Jamie told her, a warning he hoped like hell she heeded. He set his jaw and fought back a tide of angry emotion. More horrible memories from that night rushed rapid fire through his mind, making his gut clench with dread. *Leave me! You know it's over!* The backs of his lids burned.

Oh, God. He couldn't do this.

"He was a Ranger with you, right? In the same unit?"

Jamie shoved his hands into his hair, pushing it away from his face. He glanced around and realized that she'd rowed them all the way out into the middle of the lake. No escape. Panic sent acid churning though his belly. This had been a trap, he realized suddenly. She'd done this on purpose. His gaze flew to hers. Of all the sneaky, underhanded... If he wasn't so damned angry, he'd be impressed. Like a bear with a ring in its nose, she'd led him around all day, setting him up for this very moment.

And while this tactic might have worked on an ordinary man, it wasn't going to work on him, he thought grimly. He'd been a United States Ranger, by God. He was like Houdini, he could find his way out of anything.

Jamie stood, inadvertently rocking the boat.

Audrey inhaled sharply, grasped the sides.

"What are you doing? Sit down! You're going to tip us over."

"News flash, baby," Jamie told her, his lips curled in an angry smile. "Your plan didn't work."

Then he leaped neatly over the side and started swimming toward shore.

She would not break him, dammit.

She would not.

His feelings were all he had left of his friend. He didn't want to share them. And he wouldn't.

UTTERLY SHOCKED, Audrey watched Jamie determinedly swim toward shore. When she'd concocted this trap-him-in-the-boat plan, she could honestly say that she'd never anticipated this scenario. She'd wanted to force him to open up, to let her help him. The small boat had seemed like a good choice because, logistically, it would have been hard to distract her with sex, his usual, admittedly excellent, method of shutting her up.

Her eyes narrowed on his rapidly shrinking form. This new development was a setback, but she'd be damned before she'd accept defeat. The more time she spent with Jamie, the more she knew he needed her. She could feel the ache inside him worsening. Hell, he hurt so much it made *her*

nauseous. It was eating him up inside, Audrey
knew, and the more it festered, the worse it was
going to become.

She stood. "Jamie!"

When he didn't so much as look at her, Audrey
did what seemed like the only plausible thing—
she jumped in after him.

The shock of cold water stole her breath, but
she pressed on. She was an excellent swimmer,
after all, and frequently took a dip in the lake.
She'd never done it in late September, but what
the hell. New experiences were what made life
interesting. Between strokes, she looked for
Jamie and had the pleasure of seeing his out-
raged face when he saw that she'd come in after
him.

His eyes looked like they'd burst from their
sockets. "Have you lost your mind?" he shouted
at her.

Audrey ignored him. No more than he had, the
stubborn jerk. But she'd lost something a whole
lot more precious—her heart. She'd given it to a
tight-lipped obstinate former Ranger who could
swim like a friggin' fish, Audrey thought, resisting the inappropriate urge to laugh.

Jamie had doubled back and was suddenly next

to her. "Do you have a death wish?" he shouted angrily. "What the hell were you thinking?"

"I just followed your lead," she said, ignoring his anger. "I'm not letting you run away from me."

"What about the boat?"

"Fuck the boat."

His feet found ground before hers did. He gaped at her. "What is your deal?" he demanded, slogging forward. He grabbed her arm and tugged her with him.

"What's yours?" she answered back.

"I want you to lay off!"

"Why? So you can wallow in self-pity for the rest of your life?" It was risky and mean, but he wasn't mad enough yet and it was going to take anger to make him break.

Five feet from shore, his face dripping wet, clothes clinging to him like a second skin, he stopped and glared daggers at her. "Self-pity?" he repeated in a voice so quiet it was thunderous. "That's what you think is wrong with me?"

"What choice do I have when you won't level with me?"

He crossed his arms over his chest and smirked at her. "Did it ever occur to you that it was none of your damned business?"

That dart found a mark, forcing her to swallow. "Maybe not," Audrey conceded. "But you made it my business when you showed up at my camp! Sure, my grandfather ordered you here, but you didn't have to come, did you?"

He opened his mouth, readying for a comeback, but stopped short. He released a weary breath, rubbed the bridge of his nose. "Just let it go," he said instead.

Shivering, Audrey shook her head. "I won't," she told him. She thumped a hand against her chest. "I can feel it in here. It *hurts,* dammit, and if it hurts me, it's got to be killing you. Just—" She blinked, determined not to cry. "Just tell me what happened."

Jamie blanched. His gaze dropped to her chest, then darted back up and tangled with hers. She didn't have any idea what was going on in that head of his, but she could feel more and more pain radiating off him.

A helpless laugh rumbled up his throat and he shook his head. "You don't know what you're asking of me," he told her, his voice breaking.

No, she did, and that made pushing him for it even harder. Audrey fisted her hands in his shirt, looked up at him. "Nobody deserves to carry around what you're wrestling with. I may be little, but I'm tough. Share the load, Jamie," she implored, punctuating the statement with a soft kiss to his jaw.

And that did it.

Her bad-ass former Ranger closed his eyes tightly shut, rested his forehead against hers and a quiet sob shook his shoulders.

13

JAMIE FELT AUDREY'S ARMS tighten around him and he clung to her, sapping up her strength just like every other selfish bastard who'd come before him. God, he was pathetic. But he couldn't seem to help himself. She'd just kept on and on, and then when she'd told him that she could feel it too—that *his* pain was hurting *her*—that was just the last damned straw.

"Oh, Jamie," she said. She tugged him toward the cottage. "Come on. Let's go inside."

Jamie allowed her to guide him, numb from the cold, from arguing, from the grief he'd been carrying for so long. He should be taking care of her, not the other way around, and yet he wasn't strong enough to deny himself her comfort. Selfishly, he needed it. No, it was more than that—*he needed her*.

Audrey grabbed the bottle of Jameson from the

kitchen counter, then led him toward the bathroom. She quickly adjusted the tap and started the shower. One quick guzzle of whiskey later and they were both naked and under the spray. The hot water beat down like little needles of fire, warming his skin back up. She lathered him up, washing his hair in a way that was gentle but not overtly sexual. It was nice, Jamie thought, to be able to be with a naked woman—one he admittedly wanted more than any other on the planet—and yet be content not to act on that desire. He supposed that's what happened when you found the right one.

In short order, she had them both clean, warm, dressed and situated in front of a small fire. She'd tossed a couple of easy-start logs into the grate and a cozy warmth soon permeated the room.

Her hair still wet, she sat down beside him wearing one of his shirts, and offered him her hand. A simple gesture, but one that had a singularly profound effect on his heart. His throat clogged.

Okay, he thought, blowing out an uneasy breath. She wanted to know about Danny. Where to start? "You were right," Jamie told her. "Danny was in my unit. I'm assuming your grandfather told you a little bit about him and—" he cleared his throat "—what happened?"

She nodded once. "Some. He mentioned that you'd lost a good friend recently."

"That's the watered-down version." He traced a finger over her palm. Then he swallowed again. "Danny was more than a good friend. He was more like a brother. Our unit was like that. Tight. We met in college, the four of us. Me, Danny, Guy and Payne." Jamie smiled, remembering. Young and dumb, he thought, hell-bent on changing the world. "Guy and Payne are my business partners in Ranger Security," he added as an aside. The silence yawned between them, then he shook his head. "When Danny died, we... We all wanted out."

"That's certainly understandable," Audrey told him. "Surely you don't fault yourself for that?"

"No, not for that," Jamie said. "I fault myself for not saving him."

"Oh, Jamie," she sighed, smoothing the hair above his ear. "You can't fault yourself for that either."

He could and he did. Tears burned the backs of his lids, his chest ached with the pressure of guilt. Jamie swore, wiped his eyes. "I was supposed to have his back," he said, his voice cracking. "Not Payne. Not Guy. *Me*. I was the one who was supposed to make sure nothing happened to him."

In an instant, Audrey was in his lap. She straddled him, framed his face with her hands, forcing him to look her in the eye. "Jamie, your intentions were good, but we both know you were setting yourself up to do the impossible."

"But—"

She shushed him. "Let me ask you something. Did you follow procedure?"

"Of course."

"Didn't vary from what you were supposed to do and took every precautionary measure?"

"Yes, but—"

"Were you operating on good intelligence?"

She was definitely the Colonel's granddaughter, Jamie thought. He'd asked many of these same questions. "Yes."

"Then what went wrong?"

A cold chill slid down his back. "We were ambushed."

Her thumbs gently swept his cheeks. "Then how were you supposed to have his back?"

Jamie started to reply, but found he couldn't answer.

"You would have had to have been psychic to know what was going to happen," she said softly. She bent forward and kissed him, causing the flow he'd been holding back for eight months to come rushing forward in a cleansing torrent he didn't have a prayer of stopping. He cried for Danny, he cried for himself, he cried for his friends.

"Let it go," she said, hugging him tightly. She rocked him back and forth, the movement soothing and tender and heartbreakingly sweet. "I've got you," she murmured. "Just let it all go. If he was the kind of friend worthy of this grief, then he wouldn't want you holding on to it like this, would he?"

No, he wouldn't, Jamie thought. Odd how he'd never looked at it that way. It was sobering. He felt like an enormous weight had been lifted off his chest.

Audrey drew back, showered his face with healing kisses, sprinkled them along his jaw, lingered around the corner of his mouth. Jamie turned his head and caught her lips, fitted his hands on the small of her back. God, she tasted wonderful, he thought, savoring the flavor of her against his tongue. What had he ever done without her?

Knowing what he wanted—what he needed—she upped the intensity of the kiss, slid her hands down his chest, then back up again, over his neck and into his hair. An arrow of heat landed in his groin, stirring his dick beneath her.

Audrey groaned into his mouth—the sound desperate and erotic—and wriggled on top of him, rocking her hips forward to catch the ridge of his arousal. A sweet sigh stuttered out of her mouth and into his. He cupped her rump and smiled against her lips as he made a pleasant discovery—no panties. They were piled on the bathroom floor with the rest of their wet clothing.

Jamie found the hem of the shirt and tugged it up over her head, then cast it aside. Full creamy breasts crowned with rosy budded nipples. Tiny waist. A thatch of dark brown curls.

Heaven.

He bent his head forward and drew one perfect nipple into his mouth, and a commingled sigh of pleasure leaked from both his and Audrey's lungs. "I love it when you do that," Audrey told him. "I can feel it all the way down *here*," she said, rubbing herself against him. "It makes my belly all hot and muddled."

Jamie growled low in his throat as his dick

jerked beneath her. The only thing that separated him from her was a pair of boxer shorts. She leaned forward and licked a hot path up his neck, sighed into his ear, causing a wave of gooseflesh to break out over his skin. He felt a single bead of moisture leak from his dick.

She rocked against him once more, gasped as the pleasure barbed through her. "I need you," she said, her voice throaty and broken and every bit as desperate as he was.

Jamie shifted beneath her, freeing himself from his shorts and felt her warm juices slide over the swollen head of his penis.

He set his jaw and gritted his teeth.

Audrey's mouth opened in a silent O of pleasure and she moved against him once more, bumping the head of him against her clit. "God, that feels good," she told him, arching her neck back.

Jamie pushed against her, deliberately coating the length of him with her wet heat. "It can feel even better."

A sexy chuckle rattled up her throat. "Oh, I know it can," she said confidently. Then she arched herself up, positioned him at her entrance and impaled herself upon him.

A smile of sublime satisfaction transformed

her gorgeous face to something almost painfully beautiful. Her lids drooped and a gasp of sheer erotic delight slipped past her lips.

Hot, wet, tight, Jamie thought, struggling to keep from coming right then. He'd never been one to detonate upon entry, but nothing had ever felt so fabulous as the feel of Audrey's sweet little body hovering over his, balancing on his dick. He grasped her hips, thrust up, pushing himself even farther into her.

Her mouth found his once more, desperate, frantic, but confident and sure. She wasn't just making love to him, he realized, she was laying siege. For every parlay of her tongue, she rocked against him, tightened her feminine muscles. The combination made every one of his senses soar, made him buck frantically beneath her. She was everywhere. On top of his body, inside his mouth, inside his head…inside his heart.

"Oh, Jamie," she groaned, the throaty purr the sexiest thing he'd ever heard. "I'm going to— I think—"

The seed of climax had taken root, Jamie knew, upping his thrusts. He reached down between their joined bodies, found the bud nestled in the peak of her curls and stroked her.

Predictably, she went wild.

Her breath came in short broken gasps, she tightened around him, making his balls shrink and his dick threaten to explode. Jamie set his jaw and stroked her even harder. *Come on, baby,* he thought. *Give it to me so I can let it go.*

A second later, she went rigid with release, a long scream tore from her throat, and she convulsed around him. What she looked like in that instant would forever be burned into his heart. She was…amazing. A goddess.

Jamie's own release followed hers. The orgasm shot so hard from his loins, it would have blasted paint off the wall. He went weak—literally weak. His vision blackened around the edges, his breath came in ragged gasps and his legs felt like they were going to fall off.

Sweet mother.

Audrey sagged against his chest, rested her head against his shoulder and pressed a breathless kiss against his neck. "Can I tell you something?" she asked.

It took effort, but he managed to find his voice. "Sure."

"I think I'm in love with you."

Emotion clogged his throat, preventing him from immediately returning the sentiment. Danny may have died in his arms…but he'd just been reborn in hers.

14

ARMED WITH THE REMOTE and a bowl of popcorn, Audrey settled in next to Jamie on her couch. "You aren't a talker are you?"

Jamie's beer paused halfway to his mouth and he glanced at her. "What do you mean a 'talker'?"

"I mean, you aren't one of those people who has to inject commentary throughout the whole movie, right?" She faked a wince. "'Cause if you are, that's just going to ruin it for me."

He chuckled. "What? Are you going to dump me if I am?"

No, Audrey thought, shaking her head. Dumping one person today was enough, thank you very much. Rather than leave Derrick in the lurch, Audrey had taken the opportunity to call him this afternoon while Jamie had been at the camp's library selecting their movie. He'd nixed a chick flick and she'd vetoed blood and gore, so they're reached a compromise with a nice comedy.

At any rate, Derrick had been surprised by her answer to his proposal and even more shocked that she hadn't put up an argument when he'd told her that they'd simply have to break up. Thankfully, Derrick's ego was substantial enough that her refusal didn't seem to have affected him that deeply.

Still, she just felt better knowing that she'd ended that chapter in her life and started a new one with Jamie. There was nothing quite so thrilling as the blush of new romance, she thought, snuggling in next to him as the previews rolled.

Ah, Audrey thought happily. Another similarity. He didn't want to fast-forward through them.

She cast a glance at him from the corner of her eye and felt her chest squeeze with secret joy. Honestly, she could just look at him all day. Her gaze was perpetually drawn to the masculine line of his jaw, the curiously vulnerable patch of soft skin next to those amazing eyes. He just did it for her, Audrey thought. Was he perfect? No. What person was? She was suddenly reminded of a quote by Sam Keen. "You come to love not by finding the perfect person, but by seeing an imperfect person perfectly." That fit, Audrey thought, smiling softly.

And Jamie had turned a corner today. This afternoon when he'd finally broken down and shared his tragedy with her… Her own chest had ached so much it had brought tears to her eyes. He'd been grieving for so long, and worse, blaming himself. She wasn't altogether sure that he'd let himself completely off the hook in that regard, but she knew she'd argued a significant enough point to make him doubt. That was a start, at least. Baby steps, Audrey told herself, and wondered if asking him to stay with her indefinitely was more along the lines of taking a giant leap.

Technically he was supposed to go home tomorrow and yet the idea of him leaving now, after everything they'd been through this week, made her belly tip in a nauseated roll. She missed him and he hadn't even left yet. That couldn't be good, considering he was based in Atlanta and she in the wilds of Maine. Logistics, she knew, but she couldn't keep from jumping ahead.

He was it. Jamie Flanagan was The One.

"Can I ask you something?" Audrey said,

wanting to make sure they were on the same page. Or at the very least in the same chapter.

He tugged playfully on a lock of her hair. "I thought you said you didn't like to talk during the movie."

"Previews don't count."

"Ah," he sighed, inclining his head. "That's a handy piece of knowledge right there. Sure," he said in answer to her question. "Ask away."

Audrey hesitated. "Do you have to go home tomorrow?"

A slow smile tugged at the corner of his mouth and those golden green eyes softened. "Are you issuing an invitation?"

Audrey nodded. "An open one," she said, putting it all out there. In for a penny, in for a pound, she supposed.

Impossibly, those gorgeous eyes softened even more and he leaned over and brushed his lips across hers in a tender kiss that stole her breath. "I like the sound of that."

"I'm not scaring you, am I?" she asked, suddenly uncertain. She knew he cared about her—one of the only perks of this empathy thing, but… "I just—"

Jamie pressed a single finger against her mouth

and his gaze searched hers. The emotion—the unadulterated feeling he allowed her to see—made her pulse leap. "I'd only be scared if you didn't want me here."

"No worries then," Audrey told him. She leaned over and pressed her lips to his, sighed with pleasure as the innocent gesture quickly morphed into something a lot more potent. A movie? she mentally scoffed. Why watch a movie when there were other, more satisfying ways, to pass an evening.

Especially with him.

In the process of trying to crawl into his lap without upending her popcorn, Audrey jumped when a loud knock came at the door. Seconds later, it abruptly burst open.

Moses leaped off the recliner, 150 pounds of pissed-off growling canine, and barreled for the door.

"Moses, heel!" Audrey shouted at precisely the same instant she recognized her grandfather. There were two grim-faced men behind him whom she couldn't identify, but she could hardly think about them at the moment. She was more concerned with keeping her dog from ripping the Colonel's throat out. *"Heel,"* she ordered again, jumping up after the dog.

Her grandfather scowled. "Moses," he scolded. "It's only me." He glared at Jamie. "It's him you should maul."

Confused, Audrey grabbed Moses by the collar and tugged him back. "Sit," she told him, patting him on the head. Her dog issued another warning growl, but did as she commanded.

Jamie had left the couch and had come to stand behind her. "Colonel," he acknowledged. His gaze darted to the men standing behind her grandfather and he gave them an up-nod, one of those male gestures of acknowledgment which seemed to indicate that he knew them.

Baffled, Audrey tucked her hair behind her ear. "Gramps, I didn't know you were coming," she said, for lack of anything better. She hadn't called with updates the way he'd asked her to—she'd been too busy sleeping with his friend, she thought, squirming—but surely that wouldn't warrant a personal visit.

He continued to bore a hole through Jamie. "That's because I wanted the element of surprise." He paused. "When you didn't return any of my phone calls, I began to get suspicious." His brows lowered even further. "Then Tewanda made an ominous comment about 'my plan working out even better than I anticipated' and I knew that I'd created a problem."

His plan? Audrey wondered, completely confused. What plan? "Gramps, I don't under—"

"I made the mistake of contacting your friends, here, Flanagan. As you can see they leaped to the same conclusion I did and have rushed here on your behalf to try and save you. Touching, but pointless." Unbelievably, his frown grew ever darker. "Because if you have done what I think you've done—if you have rounded any of the bases I warned you about—then no one will be able to save you. I want answers," he thundered. *"Now."*

He wasn't the only one, Audrey thought, growing increasingly worried. What the hell was going on? To hell with it. She didn't have to wonder. This was her house, dammit. "Gramps, what are you talking about? Plan? Bases? Why are you threatening a guest in my home?" Granted he was her grandfather, but this was uncalled for.

For the first time since he'd barged into her home, her grandfather paused to look at her. A flash of discomfort and oddly, contrition, momentarily claimed his features. "I have a confession to make, Audie. Do you remember last week when I told you that I would always have your best interests at heart, and to always remember it?"

A cold chill settled in her belly. She looked from a grim faced Jamie back to her grandfather. "I do," she replied cautiously.

He grimaced. "Well, remember it now because what I'm about to confess is most likely going to make you angry."

"Sir," Jamie butted in, speaking for the first time since this weird scenario had begun only minutes ago. "Let me tell her. Please," he added as an afterthought.

A throb started above her left eye and a sickening sensation swept through her midsection. Tell her what? What the hell was going on?

"You lost that option, Flanagan, and you're going to lose a lot more. I trusted you with someone I love, and you betrayed that trust. You've betrayed her. You were supposed to flirt with her, dammit!" He gestured wildly. "Not treat her like all those other tramps you whore around with."

The sickening sensation worsened, pushing panic into her throat. She squeezed her eyes tightly shut. *"Gramps, what are you talking about?"*

"Flanagan owed me a favor, Audrey, and I called it in on your behalf." He shifted uncomfortably. "You see, Tewanda had told me that Derrick had proposed and I was afraid that you would say yes." He jerked his head in Jamie's direction. "He was supposed to change your mind."

Floored, Audrey didn't know what to address first, her grandfather's manipulation or Jamie's part in it. The former pissed her off and the latter... Well, the latter felt like a well-placed punch straight to her heart. "You sent a man here to seduce me?" she asked, thunderstruck. Her eyes narrowed into angry slits. "How dare—"

"Not seduce," the Colonel corrected swiftly. "He was supposed to flirt with you," he explained a bit sheepishly, unable to hold her gaze. "He was supposed to instill doubt." Her grandfather's wrath turned upon Jamie once more. "He was never supposed to touch you. Period."

Audrey went numb inside, absorbing what her grandfather had just said. She crossed her arms over her chest, chilled, and cleared her throat. "Is this true?" she asked, turning to Jamie.

"The simple answer is yes," Jamie admitted. "But I'm hoping you'll give me a chance to explain."

Audrey nodded, felt icicles lick through her

veins. Any second now she'd be frozen completely, then simply shatter. She swallowed. "I, uh…" She winced, shook her head. "I just want to be clear on something. You were supposed to change my mind about marrying Derrick and then report back to my grandfather, right? Is that the gist of it?"

Jamie nodded. "But—"

"And yet you've known the answer to that for a while, haven't you, Jamie?" He'd seduced her, knowing that she'd never intended to marry Derrick. You knew, Audrey thought. She'd pegged Jamie Flanagan as many things—fierce, loyal, competent, hers, even, and yet an opportunistic player had never been one of them. He'd used her…and she'd made it easy for him.

Evidently reading her line of thinking, Jamie stepped toward her. "Audrey, I know that you're angry and you have every right to be, but if you'll just give me a chance to explain—"

She smirked, walked between his two friends— Payne and McCann, if she remembered correctly—and opened her door. "You've had plenty of opportunities to explain, Jamie, and no one is more disappointed, or feels more foolish right now than I do." She lowered her head to hide her watering eyes. "Please go."

"Audrey," he repeated softly, a say-you-don't-mean-it tone.

She merely opened the door wider.

"WE'VE BEEN TRYING to call you," Payne told him. "To warn you. When that didn't work…" He shrugged, not stating the obvious. They'd come to his rescue. Jamie was thankful, but couldn't find the words at the moment.

"You know this isn't over with Garrett," Guy pointed out. He jerked his head toward Audrey's cottage. "Once he gets finished covering his own ass up there, he'll be down here on yours."

Jamie tossed back another shot of whiskey, hoping like hell it would warm him up inside. Seeing the look on Audrey's face when she'd realized that he'd made love to her *after* she'd given him the information he'd needed had practically flash-frozen his insides. The duplicity had been bad enough, but this… This was an even bigger betrayal.

You've had plenty of opportunities to explain, Jamie, and no one is more disappointed that you didn't or feels more foolish right now than I do.

Anger was so much easier to accept than disappointment, he thought, remembering the look of complete regret on her hauntingly beautiful face.

"Let him come," Jamie said, spoiling for a fight. Everything about this damned favor had been wrong. It was Garrett's fault. Jamie hadn't wanted to trick her to start with. He'd known then that it was wrong, that it could only end in disaster. *His.* "I've got a few things I'd like to say to him."

Guy and Payne shared a look.

"I think you'd better start figuring out a way to keep Garrett from separating your stones from your shaft, if you know what I mean," Guy suggested. "This was his *granddaughter,* Jamie." He chuckled darkly. "This wasn't just some three-date disposable girl you messed around with."

Annoyed, Jamie looked up, glared menacingly at his friend and laced his voice with unmistakable lead. "She's not disposable."

Payne's gaze sharpened. "What are you saying?"

Guy stilled, studied him for a moment. Any trace of humor vanished from his gaze. "You're in love with her, aren't you?"

Jamie nodded. "She's…it," he finally finished, releasing a pent-up breath. And he'd blown the hell out of any chance with her. "I've screwed up. I should have told her and I didn't. And she was right. I've had plenty of time, I just…" He laughed bitterly.

"You just thought she'd never have to know," Payne finished.

"Stupid bastard," Guy chimed in. "Granted I am not the authority on women that you are, but even I know they don't like being lied to."

Payne peered out the window. "Or made a fool of. She thinks she fell for an act, and the longer she ruminates on that, the harder it's going to be to change her mind."

He was right, Jamie realized. Whether she'd wanted him to leave or not, by walking away he'd just made himself look all the more guilty. What the hell had he been thinking? Had he lost his freaking mind? He didn't retreat, dammit. He'd been a Ranger, for chrissakes. He didn't back down. He'd never walked away from a fight in his life and wasn't about to start now. Not when he had so much to lose.

Namely her.

Jamie sprang up from his chair and headed toward the door.

"Where are you going?" Guy asked, startled.

"I'm taking that hill," Jamie said, referencing the old military adage. And he was prepared to die on it if need be. His lips quirked with bitter humor.

Considering Garrett wanted to kill him, that was a distinct possibility.

15

"I DON'T GIVE A DAMN why you did it, Gramps. It was wrong," Audrey told him, giving him no quarter.

"Well, I never said I was right," the Colonel replied with a self-righteous sniff. "I said I did what I thought was right. There's a difference."

Though she was angry and aching, Audrey felt a smile pull at her lips. "Are you sure you shouldn't be an attorney? Because that sounds like a load of crap to me."

"Young lady," he scolded.

"Save it," she replied firmly. "You're not going to 'young lady' me on this. You had no right to do what you did. All of this could have been avoided if you had merely asked me if I was going to marry Derrick. I would have told you."

He blinked as though the idea had never occurred to him.

"Anyway, it doesn't matter now." She stood and pushed a hand through her hair. At this point she just wanted to be alone with her thoughts and properly nurse her wounds in private. "Come on," she said. "I'll put fresh sheets in the guest bedroom."

"Oh, I've got to go have a little chat with Flanagan before I go to bed," he said with an ominous chuckle.

Audrey drew up short. "No, you don't. I forbid it."

His eyebrows soared up his forehead. "You forbid it?"

"That's right. No more meddling." Honestly, Jamie deserved nothing better than a load of brimstone from her grandfather, but she needed to set a precedent here—the Colonel had to start butting out. "You are no longer permitted to meddle in my personal affairs."

"But—"

For the second time that evening, a knock sounded at her door, then someone burst through.

Only this time that person was Jamie.

Evidently used to it by now, Moses merely lifted his head, saw that it was Jamie and lay down once more. Her grandfather, however, wasn't so relaxed.

He scowled. "What the hell do you think you're doing here?" he demanded.

His face a mask of determination, Jamie pointed a finger at him. "Stay out of it."

"*What?* Have you forgotten who you're talking to?"

"My former boss," Jamie replied smoothly. "And I didn't come here to talk to you." His gaze tangled with hers, causing the fine hairs on her arms to stand on end and an unwelcome bittersweet pang of joy to rattle her aching heart. "I came here to see you."

"Get out," the Colonel ordered.

"Hear me out, Audrey," Jamie said. "That's all I ask."

"You either get out or I'll put you out," her grandfather ordered, advancing on him.

"*I love her, dammit,*" Jamie snapped, rounding on him. "Either shut the hell up or I'll shut you up."

Audrey witnessed a phenomenon she'd never imagined she'd ever see—her grandfather speechless.

"Give us a minute, would you, Gramps?"

Though he looked like he wanted to argue, he didn't. "All right," he grumbled. He stalked to the back of the house, mumbling something under his breath about "mouthy upstarts" and "in my day…"

Had she really heard him correctly? Audrey wondered, shooting Jamie a questioning glance. Had he really just said he loved her? A hopeful sprout of happiness grew in her chest.

For the first time since he'd charged back into her living room, Jamie looked unsure of himself. It was curiously endearing.

"Audrey, I'm sorry," he said simply, the sincerest form of an apology. Regret painted his face with worry. "I'm not proud of going along with this. I just—" He paused. "I just wanted out of the military and your grandfather helped make that process easier than it should have been. I owed him. I agreed to a favor." He shook his head and his intense gaze tangled with hers. "But I never counted on anything like this. And I damned sure didn't count on coming up here and falling in love with you." He took a step toward her and grasped her shoulders. *"I love you."* A helpless laugh escaped him. "You are— You are the best thing that's ever happened to me. I know I was wrong, but— But don't cut me out over it. This evening you offered me an open invitation. Don't take it back. Please."

Audrey considered him a moment. "Why did

you make love to me when you'd already gotten the answer you were sent here to get?"

Another helpless laugh rolled out his mouth. "Because I couldn't *not* make love to you. I need you."

A tremulous smile shook her mouth. That had been the answer she'd been hoping for. And she completely understood it, because she needed him, too. She needed that crooked grin and those sexy twinkling eyes. She needed his warmth and his strength and his loyalty and integrity. All of the qualities which had made him a good soldier also made him a good partner. He'd charged up the hill and taken on her grandfather for her, Audrey thought shaking her head. Now, *that* took courage.

Jamie caressed her cheek, sending a wave of warmth and longing washing through her. Her lids fluttered shut, absorbing the feel of him.

"What do you say, Audrey? Can you forgive me?"

Audrey moved into the safe circle of his embrace, wrapped her arms around his waist, then looked up and pressed a kiss to his jaw. She smiled up at him. "Haven't you heard? I'm nothing if not forgiving."

Jamie chuckled, then lowered his mouth to hers.

"No, you're nothing if not *mine*."

Epilogue

"I WISH YOU COULD HAVE met him," Jamie said with a somber sigh. He and Audrey stood in Arlington National Cemetery, next to a plain white marble cross which marked the spot where Danny had been buried. More than a year later and Jamie was still grieving, but thanks to his wife—God, he was proud to call her that, Jamie thought, still in awe—he was allowing himself to mourn instead of blaming himself.

He glanced over his shoulder at Guy and Payne, who were standing a few markers down with the Colonel. The Colonel seemed to be in deep conversation with Payne and, judging from the unhappy look on his friend's face, he wasn't enjoying what he was hearing. Welcome to my world, Jamie thought, smiling. He didn't always enjoy his conversations with the Colonel either.

Garrett had received a commendation this morning and they'd all flown in to be there for him. Despite the interfering way he'd handled things, Jamie still owed him. The man had inadvertently introduced him to the love of his life, after all.

"I wish I could have met him, too." Audrey sighed. She squeezed his hand. "Daniel Garrett Flanagan," she announced matter-of-factly.

"What?"

"If we have a boy," she said. "We should name him after your friend and my grandfather."

It was a nice thought, but... Jamie grinned down at her. "I like it, but shouldn't we worry about that when you actually get pregnant?"

Audrey chewed the inside of her cheek, but didn't say anything.

Jamie stilled as hope leaped inside him. His heart began to race. "Audrey," he said slowly. "Are you?" he asked.

A huge grin spread across her lips and she nodded.

Jamie whooped with joy, snatched her up and whirled her around. My God, he thought. He was going to be a father. It was… It was… He shook his head. There were no words.

Except for these. "She's pregnant!" he bellowed to his baffled friends.

The Colonel beamed at them. "Audrey?" he asked for confirmation.

She nodded again. "Behave yourself and we'll name a boy after you."

Guy and Payne sidled over and slapped Jamie on the back. "Congratulations, man," Guy said, smiling. "We're honorary uncles, right?"

Jamie grinned. "Definitely."

Payne looked happy for him, but oddly distracted. And The Specialist rarely became distracted. "Is something wrong?" Jamie asked him, concerned.

"It'll keep."

"No," Jamie insisted. "You can tell me now. What's wrong?"

He glanced at Audrey, seemed to hesitate. "He just called my favor in."

So that's what they'd been talking about. "Where are you going?"

"I don't know. He's going to brief me on the return flight." He cast Audrey an uneasy look. "There aren't any more unattached women in your family I need to know about, are there?"

Audrey smiled. "Not that I know of."

Jamie laughed and wrapped an arm around Payne's shoulders. "Man, all I can say is, I hope you're as lucky with your mission as I was with mine."

Payne grimaced. From the look on his face, he hoped differently.

**Hidden in the secrets of antiquity,
lies the unimagined truth...**

Introducing

a brand-new line filled with mystery
and suspense, action and adventure,
and a fascinating look into history.

And it all begins with DESTINY.

In a sealed crypt in
France, where the
terrifying legend of
the beast of Gevaudan
begins to unravel,
Annja Creed discovers
a stunning artifact
that will seal her destiny.

*Available every other
month starting
July 2006, wherever
you buy books.*

**Four sisters.
A family legacy.
And someone is out to destroy it.**

A captivating new limited continuity, launching June 2006

The most beautiful hotel in New Orleans,
and someone is out to destroy it. But mystery,
danger and some surprising family revelations
and discoveries won't stop the Marchand sisters
from protecting their birthright...
and finding love along the way.

Page-turning drama…

Exotic, glamorous locations…

Intense emotion and passionate seduction…

Sheikhs, princes and billionaire tycoons…

This summer, may we suggest:

THE SHEIKH'S DISOBEDIENT BRIDE
by Jane Porter

On sale June.

AT THE GREEK TYCOON'S BIDDING
by Cathy Williams

On sale July.

THE ITALIAN MILLIONAIRE'S VIRGIN WIFE

On sale August.

With new titles to choose from every month,
discover a world of romance in our books written
by internationally bestselling authors.

Silhouette®

BOMBSHELL™

The Marian priestesses were destroyed long ago,
but their daughters live on. The time has come
for the heiresses to learn of their legacy, to unite
the pieces of a powerful mosaic and bring light to
a secret their ancestors died to protect.

The Madonna Key

Follow their quests each month.

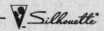